IT'S ABOUT BRIDGES

In Search of "Zoi" (Greek for "Life") - Volume III

Leaders Matter: Why Elections are Crucial

GEORGE GEORGALIS

ISBN: 979-8-3304-6888-1 (sc)
ISBN: 979-8-3304-6889-8 (e)

2024.10.09

This book is printed on acid-free paper.

georgegerogalis.com

IT'S ABOUT BRIDGES

In Search of "Zoi" (Greek for "Life") - Volume III

Leaders Matter: Why Elections are Crucial

FOREWORD

This book uses experiences gained in three wars to identify the dangers to our world and freedoms in the 21st Century.

"Conceived in Grecian thought, strengthened by Christian morality, and stamped indelibly into American political philosophy, the right of the individual against the State is the keystone of our Constitution."

(Quote from John F. Kennedy, 35th President of the USA)

The people of the World have been guided by *"rules for living"* since the ***"Ten Commandments"*** of Moses some 3,400 years ago, followed by the standard bearing Year 1215 ***"Magna Carta"*** of Great Britain and the 1787 "***United States Constitution***." These documents provide guidance for *"freedom"* and *"the pursuit of happiness"* to nations that adopt them.

"The US Constitution performs an important role in American history and the spread of democratic ideals around the world."

We list below the key elements of the US Constitution and hi-lite the two key provisions that serve the purposes of this book. The Constitution:

- **Creates a government that puts the power in the hands of the people**
- Separates the powers of government into three branches: the legislative branch, which makes the laws; the executive branch, which executes the laws; and the judicial branch, which interprets the laws
- Sets up a system of checks and balances that ensures no one branch has too much power
- Divides power between the states and the federal government

- Describes the purposes and duties of the government
- Defines the scope and limit of government power
- **Prescribes the system for electing representatives**
- Establishes the process for the document's ratification and amendment
- Outlines many rights and freedoms of the people.

"Marxism-Communism and radical Islamic philosophies are evil and harm the world"

The history of mankind has overwhelmingly proven the failures of Marxism-Communism and radical Islamists ideologies.

- There were over 60 million deaths between 1917 and 1945 from the wars against Hitler's National-Socialism and Stalin's Communism.
- The September 11, 2001 radical Islamist strikes at New York's World Trade Center and the Pentagon caused the deaths of 2,996 people and were the deadliest terrorist attacks in human history.
- Radical Islamists savagely murdered 1200 Israelis and took 251 hostages at the October 7, 2023 invasion of Israel.
- Our current millennial generation seems to have forgotten the Berlin wall and the *"Iron Curtain"* fences erected by Communists to keep Eastern Europe citizens from escaping to the West.
- The failures of the Communist *"redistribution of wealth"* philosophy caused the long lines in Eastern Europe between 1945-1991, as people waited for the food and clothing that never appeared in the Communist marketplace.

"Legal voting is crucial to selecting leaders."

- We need to encourage the citizens of nations, and especially US citizens, to vote. There are despot rulers in our world who acquire or remain in power by denying the right of their citizens to select their leaders.

- This book exposes how radical Islamists and Marxist regimes in today's world deny their citizens the right to choose leaders. We will look at the 2024 elections in Russia, Venezuela and the United States to show how Marxist regimes rig elections.

"New Book Warns of National Peril: Volume III – Leaders Matter: Why Elections are Crucial"

The following Press Release provides the reason for my writing, and for you to read, this book.

- In a new book released in October 2024, author George S. Georgalis sounds a clarion call to action. He urges American citizens to vote in the forthcoming election. He believes American citizens hold the power to affect change by selecting leaders who can restore America as *"One Nation under God,"* and return the USA to its traditional roles of protecting the oppressed and restoring peace in the world. He uses the metaphor of a bridge to represent a nation. A strong foundation built on shared values is essential, but a *"crooked deck"* placed on the superstructure can lead to disaster. The author contends that's what transpired in the 2020 US election, with fraudulent votes and voting machines enabling a *"crooked regime"* to plot a *"crooked path"* and take control of our Nation.

- The author warns of the dangers in the 21st-century posed by threats from Communism and radical Islam. He shares experiences from three prior wars to show that wars are fought not just on earth, but in the mind and from the heavens as well.

- Mr. Georgalis has written a prior book ***"It's About Bridges, Volume IIB – The Education and War Stories"*** that has garnered positive reviews on Amazon.com, boasting an impressive 4-star average rating. A 5-star review by Sol Tyler effusively praises the book as *"A breathtaking piece of cinematic art itself. I consider it a great and smart read with really interesting information for all of us to enjoy. The action hops around what the author thinks was fraud during the 2020 election, and the narrative gets so interesting as soon as the story flows that all sorts of readers would be able to enjoy it. The events in It's About Bridges lead us to an entirely original structure, which makes it a ground-breaking, mystic literary, and almost cinematic experience. The book also gave me* *much food for thought about what is or may be happening in the adult world today. It is outstanding!"*

- Both of the books, ***"It's About Bridges, Volume IIB – The Education and War Stories"*** and **"Volume III – Leaders Matter: Why Elections are Crucial,"** are directed to a specific audience: **You**. Mr. Georgalis believes ordinary citizens hold the power to affect change. He urges readers to vote, and to embrace their leadership potential by answering the call when the time comes. By picking up either of the ***"It's About Bridges"*** books, you're not just reading a book; ***"you're taking up the torch of freedom."*** Georgalis equips readers with the knowledge and inspiration to become active participants in shaping the destiny of their nation. Both books are available for purchase on Amazon and other major book retailers.

A SEARCH FOR LEADERS AND HEROES

These are troubling times in the world, particularly in Russia, Venezuela and the United States. These nations are coping with 2024 presidential elections. These nations are in need of a **Leader** to appear from the voting, with the hope that a government ***"by the people"*** rather than ***"by a despot"*** will emerge. I also have experienced a search for a **Leader**. Let me begin this book by sharing that experience with you.

TABLE OF CONTENTS

CHAPTER I

A Visit To Salisbury England

Leaders are not merely defined as human beings, but can also be found in the writings of history which guide us through life's journey. My search for a **Leader** thus began when my family and I visited the United Kingdom for a November 2019 Thanksgiving celebration. We stopped at the world-famous gothic **Salisbury Cathedral**, located 70 miles south-west of the Heathrow airport, on our return trip to London. The **Leader** I was seeking could be found in a parchment stored in the **museum section** of the **Salisbury Cathedral.** I accompanied my family into the Salisbury town center for a tour, and later for a meal at one of a chain of restaurants uniquely named the ***"Boston Tea Party"*** **Inn.** This particular ***Boston Tea Party,*** nestled in the heart of **Salisbury,** is located in a former English historical building appropriately named ***"The Old George Inn."*** That inn dates back to the early **1300s** and once boasted the likes of **William Shakespeare**, **Oliver Cromwell** and **Samuel Pepys** among its guests. It was at this historic inn that I initiated my search for a leader - by entering the museum section of the Salisbury Cathedral - where one of the four original copies of the **Magna Carta** is located.

1. The *"Sergei Skripal Incident"* in Salisbury. As I left the **Boston Tea Party Inn** that 30 November 2019 evening, on my way to the **Salisbury Cathedral**, I walked past **Zizzi's restaurant** on Castle Street and the **Bishops Mill Pub** in the town center. Both 66-year old **Sergei Skripal** and his 33-year-old daughter **Yulia** had visited **Zizzi's** and the **Bishops Mill Pub** on 4 March 2018, just before they were found by a passing doctor and nurse ***"slipping in and out of consciousness"*** on a public bench in the town center. They had been poisoned by Russian agents of the ***"FSB"*** (the Russian security agency and former Soviet ***"KGB")*** to permanently ***silence*** whatever their role had been in a renewal of the intelligence segment of the former ***"Cold War."*** **Sergei Skripal** is a former Russian military officer. He was a double agent for the United Kingdom's Intelligence Services from 1995 until his arrest in Moscow in December 2004. In August 2006, he was convicted of high treason and sentenced to 13 years in a penal colony by a Russian court. The British arranged for his exit from Russia in 2010 as part of a spy swap. This allowed Sergei, who holds dual Russian and British citizenship, to settle into Salisbury, where he had presumed himself safe from Russian persecution, until that fateful day of 4 March 2018. A ***"Novichok nerve agent,"*** used by the FSB as poison, was so powerful that just a ***drop*** placed on someone's clothing would be lethal. That's what happened to **Sergei** and **Yulia Skripal** on 4 March 2018.

a. The perfume bottle in Amesbury. Let's look at what later transpired on 30 June 2018 in **Amesbury**, seven miles from **Salisbury**, after investigators found a perfume bottle containing ***"Novichok"*** where it had been disposed of in a garbage bin. A man innocuously found and gave that perfume bottle containing the nerve agent to **Dawn Sturgess**. She sprayed it on her wrist, fell ill within 15 minutes and died on 8 July. A later chemical analysis of that perfume bottle determined it contained enough of the ***Novichok*** nerve agent to potentially kill thousands of people. The search for more evidence of Russia misdeeds was underway. On 13 March 2018, UK Home Secretary **Amber Rudd** ordered an inquiry by the police and security services into alleged Russian state involvement in 14 previous suspicious deaths of Russian exiles and businessmen in the United Kingdom. More evidence piled up, too much to list here, which mandated some ***response*** to the Russians. Also, **Western Europe** still had not adequately dealt with ***"Russian adventurism"*** in the **Ukraine**.

b. The aftermath of the *"Sergei Skripal incident."* Europe's answer to Russian expansion into Ukraine, and the poisoning of **Sergei Skripal** and his 33-year-old daughter **Yulia,** was a limited and futile expulsion of 153 Russian diplomats from 28 countries, with further ***economic sanctions*** against Russia. These were all rather ineffective, vs. a military deterrent, to motivate Russia to stop assassinations of Russia defectors and to withdraw from Crimea and the Donbas region of Ukraine. What the naïve European leaders of today cannot fathom is that Russia will **never voluntarily** get out of the Donbas, or return annexed **Crimea** to the Ukraine.

2. Is Sergei Skripal a Leader or Hero? While Sergei Skripal was a key constituent of the intelligence portion of the European ***"Cold War,"*** his categorization as a **"leader"** or ***"hero"*** requires a closer look into the predominant conflicts of the 21st Century. These conflicts are mostly political, and involve the existential struggles within Russia and the United States to sustain the current leaders and ruling political parties of both nations.

CHAPTER II

The Leaders and Political Systems of the 21st Century

As evident by the Sergei Skripal incident, Russia and the Western world/United States have re-entered the ***"Cold War"*** which surfaced after World War II and disappeared with the dissolution of the Soviet Union in 1991. Both the USA and Russia have elections scheduled in the Year 2024 to determine the fate of their existing leaders. The ruling parties of both nations are intent on retaining power. Let's review how they do that. Let's begin by taking a closer look at how both the USA and Russia have replaced TRUTH with LIES to enable their leaders to attain and sustain power.

1. The contributions of Dr. Joseph Goebbels, the propaganda minister of Nazi Germany, to our search for leaders. Dr. Goebbels served Adolf Hitler as the Nazi propaganda minister from 1933 until 1945. During this time, he used the **Goebbels Doctrine** to ***"control the minds of the German folk."*** It involves just two sentences, and is supplemented by his clarification of how a dictatorial state must use LIES rather than TRUTH to govern. Those two sentences are:

"Tell lies long enough to where people believe they are true"
and
"Accuse the other side of that for which you are guilty."

Dr. Goebbels then explains that ***TRUTH is the mortal enemy of the LIE, and the greatest enemy of a State which uses the LIE to govern.*** A photograph of Dr. Goebbels, superimposed with his doctrinal quotes, is copied below:

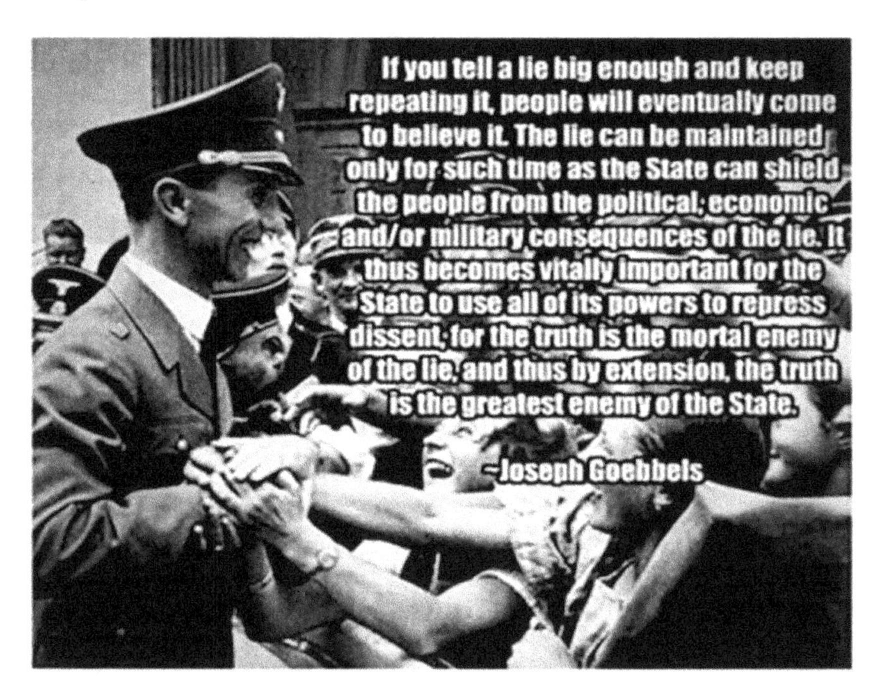

2. The Contributions of the Magna Carta and the Salisbury Cathedral to our search for Leaders. Upon my November 2019 entry into the museum section of the Salisbury Cathedral, I headed straight to a tent which contains the original copy of the Year 1204 **Magna Carta.** Then, taking advantage of the *"magic"* made possible and even encouraged by being an author, I erected an imaginary stand next to the Magna Carta tent, where I placed copies of the **Communist Manifesto**, the **Bible** and the **Quran**. I now had all of the potential literary ***"Leaders"*** from the writings of history directly visible in front of me, and can now describe how these ***"Leaders"*** might influence us.

The tent shielding the Magna Carta within the
museum of the Salisbury Cathedral.

- **The Magna Carta** was a document signed by **King John** at **Runnymede England** in **1215.** It established a number of important principles which have been copied around the world, including within the US Constitution and the Universal Declaration of Human Rights. The main points of the Magna Carta are: ***1) No one is above the law, not even the king; 2) Everyone has a right to a fair trial; and 3) No taxation without representation.***

Manifest

Kommunistischen Partei.

MANIFESTO

COMMUNIST PARTY

CHICAGO

COMPANY

Original cover of the 1848 Marx/Engels Communist Manifesto from Germany (left side) with the English translation of 1913 (right side).

- The **Communist Manifesto,** published in February **1848** in the City of **London**, is the keystone document for **Marxism**. The Manifesto justifies violence to bring its principles into power. The guidance found on **page 23** of the **Manifesto** calls for the ***"Forcible overthrow of all existing social conditions"*** and ***"Communist revolutions around the world."***

Bible displayed alongside the Quran on a table at Salisbury.

- **The Bible** contains the 10 commandments handed down by God to Moses 3,400 years ago at Mount Sinai. It is the original Constitution which provides the ***"rules of living"*** for those of the Judao-Christian faith

- **A Quran verse** is used by radical elements of Islam to justify the application of terror against non-believers. It is in **Chapter 9 Verse 5** where one finds: ***"And when the forbidden months have passed, kill the idolaters wherever you find them and take them prisoners, and beleaguer them, and lie in wait for them at every place of ambush. But if they repent and observe Prayer and pay the Zakat, then leave their way free. Surely, Allah is Most Forgiving, Merciful."***

CHAPTER III

The Education

The most difficult part of this book is my feeble attempt to explain that Wars are fought not just on **Earth**, but in the **Mind** and **Heavens** as well. But I have to try. Please bear with me.

1. The Earthly War Theater. We'll begin by talking about the Earthly War Theater, where wars are fought using weapons that follow Sir Isaac Newton's Laws.

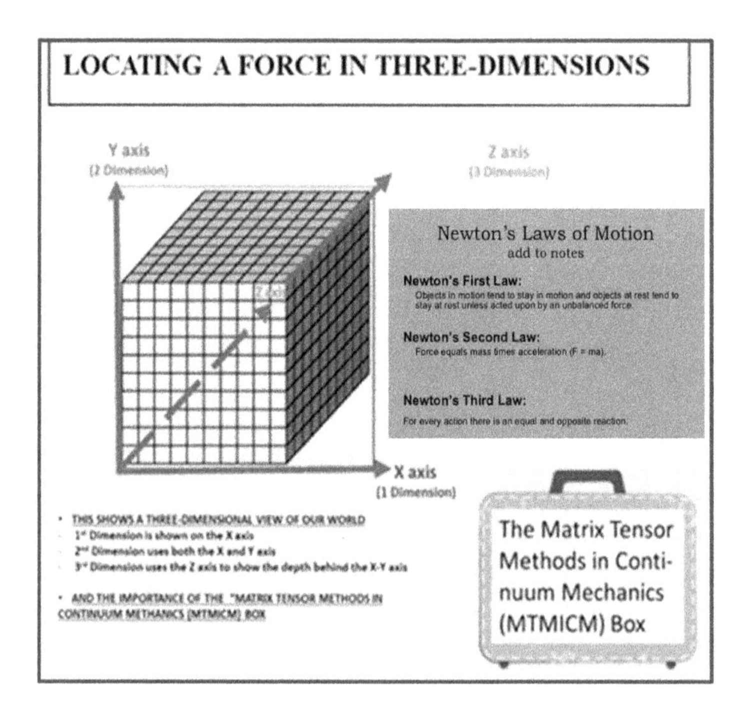

- The **Newton's Laws of Motion** chart at the right lists the three laws which are fundamentals to both **physical forces** *(forces in our Earthly Wars)* and **logical arguments** *(forces in our Mind Wars).* I was exposed to these forces when I was learning about bridge-building in a 1960s University of Kentucky structures class. I had no problem understanding the first and second dimensional forces, but had great difficulty understanding forces in the third dimension.

a. The "*MTMICM*" box in the Search for Truth in Three Dimensions.

- Please note that ***little green box*** located at the bottom right of the **Three Dimensions** chart. I call it the ***Matrix Tensor Methods in Continuum Mechanics (MTMICM)*** box**.** I gotta add a long story to explain how I discovered what it is. It happened in May 1966 during my last semester in school. I only needed one ***"required three-hour Engineering course"*** to graduate, and that was the ***MTMICM*** course. It was as difficult as the title, and I was ***not getting it.*** The best thing about the course however, was the instructor **Dr. Adams**. He was excellent in both what he taught and how he ***connected*** with students, the kind of instructor that every student should have. All I had to do was pass a ***final exam*** in Dr. Adam's **MTMICM** course to graduate. Although I believed everything Dr. Adams taught in three-dimensional forces and structures, I never fully understood it, as it was way too complicated. The night before the final exam, my final ***candle*** burned out. I couldn't even open the **MTMICM** book. So I went into that final exam ***stone cold flat*** – i.e. ***I didn't even crack the book or study at all for a class that I had to pass to graduate!*** Then a miracle began to happen as we sat for the final exam. First Dr. Adams said we could ***"take the final exam and that would be our grade for the class; or, we could take the grade we already earned with our mid-term exam and skip taking the final."*** You already know what our class would decide. Then Dr. Adams wrote all 12 of our mid-term number grades on the board. You could see a ***break in the grades*** where an **A** might be, **B** might be, etc. My grade was somewhere down between a low **D** and **F**, i.e. ***failing!*** Then Dr. Adams asked the class where to put the ***grade lines.*** I'll never forget **Joey Woolums**. He suggested that since this was a graduate level course, then all we had to do was to decide who got ***As*** and who got ***Bs.*** **I GOT A B! I GRADUATED THE NEXT DAY!**

- So why this story? Because ever since, whenever I would run across a **TRUTH** too complicated to understand, or if I was ***too dumb*** to figure it out, I would put that **TRUTH** in my mental ***"MTMICM box."*** I would take it out of the ***box*** and dust it off only if I had to. What is scary though, while preparing this book - ***I found the textbook for that class was still around – like a vampire that never dies!*** Don't believe me? Here's an ad for that horrible book listed on the **Amazon** web page – just to prove this ***vampire*** from **1966** is still around in **2020!**

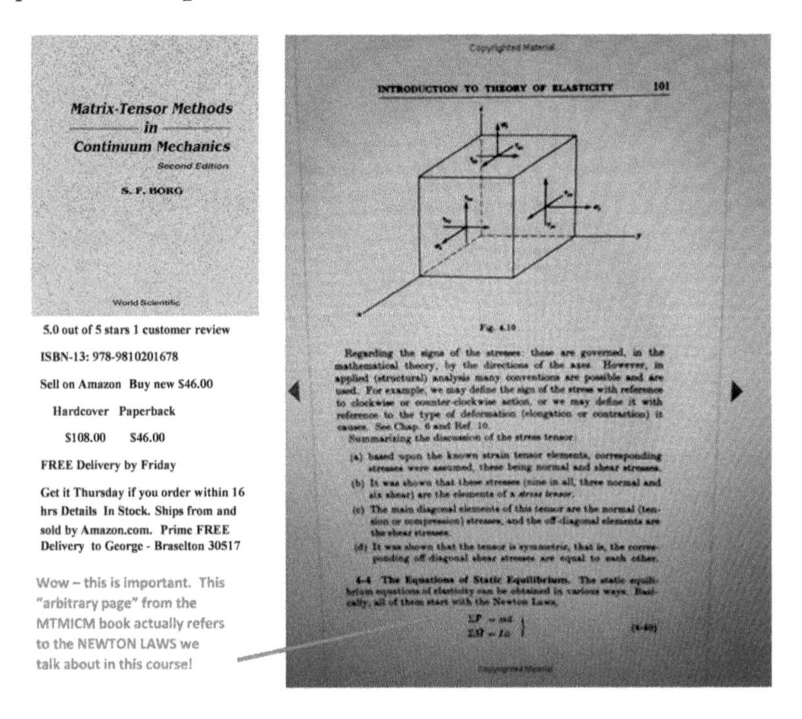

INTRODUCTION TO THEORY OF ELASTICITY 101

Fig. 4.10

Regarding the signs of the stresses: these are governed, in the mathematical theory, by the directions of the axes. However, in applied (structural) analysis many conventions are possible and are used. For example, we may define the sign of the stress with reference to clockwise or counter-clockwise action, or we may define it with reference to the type of deformation (elongation or contraction) it causes. See Chap. 6 and Ref. 10.

Summarizing the discussion of the stress tensor:

(a) based upon the known strain tensor elements, corresponding stresses were assumed, these being normal and shear stresses.

(b) It was shown that these stresses (nine in all, three normal and six shear) are the elements of a *stress tensor*.

(c) The main diagonal elements of this tensor are the normal (tension or compression) stresses, and the off-diagonal elements are the shear stresses.

(d) It was shown that the tensor is symmetric, that is, the corresponding off-diagonal shear stresses are equal to each other.

4-4 The Equations of Static Equilibrium. The static equilibrium equations of elasticity can be obtained in various ways. Basically, all of them start with the Newton Laws,

$$\left.\begin{array}{l}\Sigma F = ma\\ \Sigma M = I\alpha\end{array}\right\} \quad (4\text{-}40)$$

b. The Faith Box.

- We also need some way to deal with the **Descartes Emotional Laws** that we can't understand, kinda like the **MTMICM** box where we store complicated **Newton's Motion Laws.** Let's go over first what made **Rene Descartes** famous. He was an early 17 Century mathematician and physicist, but he also got into what happens in your head. He has been heralded as the first modern philosopher. He made a connection between geometry and algebra to prove the existence of, and therefore the reality of, ***emotions*** and ***things*** we **can't** see. His ***"I THINK, THEREFORE, I AM"*** conclusion to his research was the founding principal which, by doubting his existence, he conclusively proves that we really do exist! That's why **DesCartes** is as important as **Newton** in our study of **TRUTHS**, especially **TRUTHS** that are **not** visible. And that's why we created a ***"Faith Box,"*** similar to the Newtonian Motion Laws ***"MTMICM Box,"*** to handle **Descartes** complicated ***"Logical and Emotional Truths/Thoughts"*** beyond our understanding.

- Dr. Mark Gungor explanation of Emotion. Dr. Gungor is a pastor, motivational speaker and author who uses humor to explain complex psychological theories. He has a ***marriage counseling*** presentation to describe ***Emotional Energies*** as the differences between how men and women think. Extracts of his marriage counseling pitch follow. *(Note the **FAITH BOX** in the bottom right corner of the below **Gungor** graphic. It is used to store those difficult EMOTIONS described by DesCartes, and is similar to the **MTMICM Box** we described earlier. You will later see both the **MTMICM** and **FAITH Boxes** used as **"picnic boxes"** on a trip over the **"bridge of knowledge"** in our search for truths beyond our three-dimensional world).*

SEARCH FOR TRUTH USING LAWS OF LOGIC AND EMOTION

(mostly from Mark Gungor Marriage Counseling Lectures, www.markgungor.com)

GEN LIVSEY ALLOWED DR MARK GUNGOR TO DO THIS

- We're gonna start discussing men's brains and women's brains
- Now women's brains are very very different than men's brains
- Women's brains are made up like a big ball of wire
- And every thing is connected to EVERYTHING
- It's like the internet superhighway, OK?
- It's one of the reasons that women seem to care about EVERYTHING and to remember EVERYTHING
- And it's all driven by energy we call EMOTION
- The same thing happens for men; it just doesn't happen very often
-Men's brains are made up of little boxes
- And when we discuss something, we go to that particular box
-We have a box in our brain that we call the NOTHING box. And of all the boxes we have, this is our FAVORITE box
-And if Women stored things in "boxes' like men, this would be their EMOTION box, or FAITH box

A FAITH BOX, for storing EMOTIONS such as LOVE and HATE

2. The Heavenly War Theater. We're now about to look into the ***Heavenly War Theater***, where a **CREATOR** and **DESTROYER** are involved in an eternal conflict that ***makes the world and universe go around***. The ***equal and opposite*** energies from that encounter are the secrets to creating and maintaining an ***ever-changing*** and ***never-changing*** Universe. ***Don't try too hard to understand that last sentence***. Please know that you're getting this from someone who is not a learned scholar or scientist, but just a person trying to explain the unexplainable. We all accept that ***Forces*** and ***Energies*** exist in our Universe. We can't know what ***"form"*** they take. It is therefore easier for us to think of them as resembling ***persons,*** such as "***Archangels***" or "***Power Authorities,***" who toss these energies into the Valley of Life as ***inanimate objects*** that look like ***"lightning bolts."*** That's why we are bringing our **MTMICM** and **FAITH** boxes with us on this trip, as we will need them to store unexplainable and too hard-to-understand concepts.

- We begin our trip using the following chart. It shows a ***fox,*** who represents ***us,*** walking down the path of life. He's about to jump into the ***Valley of Life*** in ***search of "Zoi"*** *(Greek for* ***"Life"****)* when he observes the twin mountain peaks on the other side of the valley. Those mountains represent the ***CREATOR*** and ***DESTROYER*** forces that come from ***beyond our 3-D world.*** Therefore, before he jumps into the ***Valley of Life***, the *fox* needs to learn more about those forces that impact life that come from ***beyond the 3 Dimensions of our world.***

PATHWAYS AND LANDMARKS IN THE JOURNEY FOR TRUTH

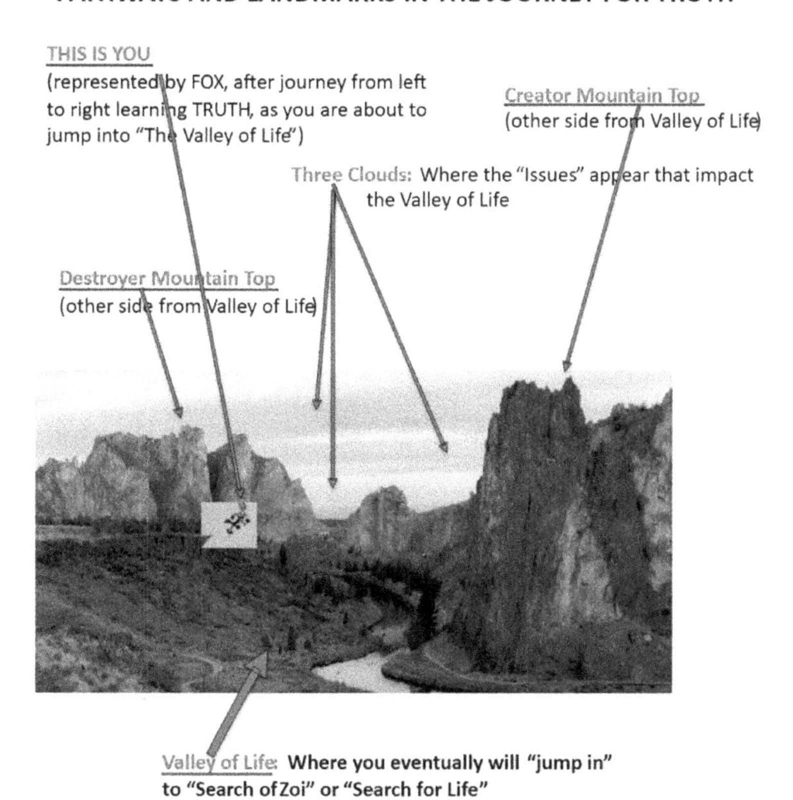

- The following chart shows two persons crossing over the ***bridge of knowledge*** to get to the other side to look for **TRUTHS** ***beyond our Earthly three-dimensional knowledge***. Note they are taking the ***MTMICM*** and ***FAITH picnic boxes*** on that trip. These boxes are where they can store the unexplainable or too difficult **Newtonian** and **DesCartes Truths** they might come across on their journey.

CROSSING THE VALLEY OF LIFE FOR A PICNIC "ON THE OTHER SIDE"
IN SEARCH OF TRUTH BEYOND THREE DIMENSIONS

NOTE YOU ARE TAKING YOUR PICNIC BASKETS WITH YOU

- **The "Matrix Tensor Methods in Continuum Mechanics" (MTMICM) Box**
where questionable knowledge is stored involving the **LAWS OF NEWTON.**
- **The "FAITH" Box**
Where questionable knowledge is stored involving **EMOTIONS** such as **HATE and LOVE**

- The next chart shows our educational picnic as an outdoor classroom. We're in a ***beyond three dimensional*** or ***4th Dimensional*** part of the world. We're looking into the ***Heavenly War Theater***, where the **CREATOR** and **DESTROYER** sides of the ***Twin Mountain Peaks*** are involved in that eternal conflict that ***makes the world and universe go around***. The ***equal and opposite*** energies from that encounter are the secrets to creating and maintaining an

ever-changing and ***never-changing*** Universe. That's why we brought our two **MTMICM** and **Faith** picnic baskets on this ***field trip picnic*** where we can deposit and store unexplainable ***TRUTHS.***

SIR ISAAC NEWTON PREPARES US FOR THE PICNIC QUEST FOR TRUTH

Sir Isaac Newton
(25 Dec 1642 – 20 Mar 1726/27)
English mathematician, astronomer, theologian, author and physicist widely recognized as one of the most influential scientists of all time

• NEWTON'S THIRD LAW OF MOTION: FOR EVERY ACTION, THERE IS AN EQUAL AND OPPOSITE REACTION.

• HOW DOES NEWTON'S LAW AFFECT OUR SEARCH FOR TRUTH
(all of this has to go into our MTMCM and FAITH boxes)
- If there is a GOD (Good), then there is an equal and opposite EVIL (Devil)
- If one of the "mountain tops" representGOD, or the CREATOR, then the other "mountain top" representsEVIL, or the DESTROYER
- If Newton's Law applies, then the "left mountain top" that represents GOD/CREATOR has a strength that is EQUAL and OPPOSITE to the "right mountain top" representing EVIL/DESTROYER. WHEW!!!!

• HOW DO THE MOUNTAIN TOPS AFFECT US?
- Each mountain top has a box of lightning bolts that represent forces. They toss these into the VALLEY OF LIFE to impact us.
- These "lightning bolts" are also EQUAL and OPPOSITE in strength;
-- For the CREATOR lightning bolt of LIFE, the DESTROYER has a DEATH lightning bolt
-- If the CREATOR has a lightning bolt representingLOVE; then the DESTROYER has HATE.
-- If the CREATOR has MORAL; the DESTROYER has DECADENT
- One last thought? These "lightning bolts" never come directly into the "Valley of Life," hence we can't tell if they come from the "Good" side or the "Bad" side of the Mountain. No, the lightning bolts are delivered instead into "clouds" – where issues appear – and no one can see whether the "issue" is influenced by a GOOD or BAD bolt.

- The last graphic below shows the 10 *"Lightning Bolts"* that can land in our **Valley of Life**. They can come at us either as ***"single-pointed"*** bolts or "***dual-edged***" bolts. We might be able to understand the ***"single-pointed"*** lightning bolts. But the "***dual-edged"*** Lightning bolts come at us through clouds which hide the lightning bolts origin, from either the ***"Creator"*** or "***Destroyer"*** part of the Heavens, and denies the recipients of the *"Lightning Bolt"* from knowing which *"edge"* of the bolt has hit them.

- This is how **LOVE** might be replaced by **HATE** in the interrelation of nations and peoples.

- This is how the pursuit of **LIFE,** through regeneration-of-the-species and rules-for-living, is replaced by **DEATH** through abortion-of-unborns and murders from wars and terror.

- A **MORAL** existence based upon the laws of God and man might be replaced by the **DECATENT** pursuit of drugs, deviant sexual practices, and pornographic ventures.

- This is how **HEALTH** through living and medicine is replaced by **ILLNESS** through Covid-19 pandemics and diseases.

- This is how the **TRUTH** and **FAKE-FALSE** can be clouded in the minds of our students, who demonstrate their believe that Hamas is the oppressed victim of Israel, and that the 7 October 2023 Hamas slaughter of 1200 innocent civilians and the taking of 251 hostages from Israel did not happen.

And because we have no control or knowledge that effects the dual-edged *"hits"* from the Heavenly Theater, we don't know which edge of the Lightning bolts hit us.

HOW THE LIGHTNING BOLTS TRAVEL THRU 'CLOUDS' TO THE VALLEY OF LIFE
CREATOR MOUNTAIN SIDE
of GOD/GOOD/LIGHT
(Christian-Judeo/Muslim/Hindu)
(All Other Religions)
DESTROYER MOUNTAIN SIDE
of DEVIL/EVIL/DARK
(Secular-Socialists)
(Radical Muslims)
(All Other Evils)
Love Life Moral Health Truth
Hate Death Decadent Illness Fake-False
"Clouds"
Love
Life
Moral
Health
Truth
Hate
Death
Decadent
Illness
Fake-False
This is the "Heavenly War Theater" and the "Valley of Life" where we conduct our "Search for Zoi," and where we have little influence on the landing of the LIGHTNING BOLTS from the "Beyond 3-D World."

CHAPTER IV

A Comparison of How the USA and Russia Govern in The 21st Century

The replacement of **TRUTH** with **LIES** is the key to governance by both Russia and the USA in the decade of the 2020s. So let's explore how both nations employ elements of the ***"Goebbels Doctrine"*** to govern and conduct elections, beginning with how this is done in Russia.

1. PUTIN'S LEADERSHIP OF RUSSIA SINCE THE YEAR 2000. The 23-year rule of Russia by Vladimir Putin has witnessed the use of ruthlessness to silence Putin's opponents. Throughout his rule, Kremlin critics, journalists and defected spies have been eliminated for opposing the Russian president. The form of attacks varied, from underwear daubed with nerve agent ***"Novichok"*** and polonium-laced tea to more straightforward assassinations by bullet. Let's look at some of them.

a. Shootings. While poison has emerged as the weapon of choice in Putin's Russia, several Kremlin critics have also been mysteriously suicidal or shot dead over the years.

- In 2006, **Anna Politkovskaya**, a Novaya Gazeta journalist who reported on human rights abuses, was killed outside her flat in Moscow after returning home from the supermarket.

- In 2013, **Boris Berezovsky** was found apparently hanged in the bathroom of his Ascot home in England. Berezovsky was a former Kremlin insider turned vocal critic of Putin's government who went into self-imposed exile in the UK in the early 2000s. Many of Berezovsky's associates have also died in mysterious circumstances, including **Badri Patarkatsishvili**, a Georgian oligarch and business partner, and **Nikolai Glushkov** and the Yukos oil founder **Yuri Golubev**, two associates who were found dead in London.

- Arguably the most brazen killing was the assassination of **Boris Nemtsov**, a prominent opposition leader, in central Moscow in 2015. Nemtsov was shot four times in the back by an unknown assailant within view of the Kremlin. A joint investigation from ***the Insider***, ***the BBC*** and ***Bellingcat*** revealed that Nemtsov had been shadowed by FSB agents for almost a year before he was assassinated on a bridge.

- While most political assassinations have occurred on Russian soil, Moscow has also been accused of shooting its opponents abroad. Most notably, in the summer of 2019, **Zelimkhan Khangoshvili,** a Georgian citizen who fought against Russia during the Chechen war in the early 2000s, was shot twice in the head at close range in the Kleiner Tiergarten park in central **Berlin**.

- Another former Kremlin insider, **Mikhail Lesin**, who founded the English-language television network ***RT***, formerly ***Russia Today***, was discovered dead in a hotel room in **Washington DC** in 2015, where he had been invited to attend a fundraising dinner. Once a power player in Putin's rise to power, **Lesin** was surprisingly dismissed from his position in the Kremlin's influential media apparatus. After a lengthy investigation, a US autopsy concluded he died as a result of "blunt force injuries" and not a heart attack, as the Russian state media had reported.

- One mystery that will likely remain unsolved is the death of **Kirill Stremousov**, the Russia-installed deputy governor of Kherson province in **Ukraine**, who according to Russian officials, died in a car crash on the day Ukrainian forces liberated Kherson in the autumn of 2022.

b. Intimidation. Putin is assured re-election as Russian President in the March 2024 election. Evidence of that appeared in a Feb 6, 2024 Atlanta news article discussing a challenger to Putin in the March 2024 elections. The Russians will eventually doom his candidacy. Extracts from that article follow: **Challenger to Putin brings rare show of defiance.** Thousands of people across Russia are signing petitions to support the long-shot candidacy of **Boris Nadezhdin**, a 60-year-old legislator and academic. His campaign has struck a chord with the public, openly calling for a halt to the conflict in Ukraine, the end of mobilizing Russian men for the military and starting a dialogue with the West. He also has criticized the country's repression of LGBTQ+ activism. He has become a problem for the Kremlin in the March presidential election. The question now is whether Russian authorities will allow him on the ballot. **Nadezhdin's** campaign got a boost after opposition leaders abroad, including former tycoon **Mikhail Khodorkovsky** and supporters of imprisoned opposition politician **Alexei Navalny**, urged Russians to support any candidate who could deny Putin a share of the vote. The election is the first since Putin annexed four Ukrainian regions and the first in which online voting will be used. Critics suggest that both are opportunities to rig results in favor of Putin. Analysts say the election's outcome is a foregone conclusion, and that Putin will stay in power for another six years. The Central Election Commission could declare the petitions invalid and bar **Nadezhdin** from the ballot. Authorities could also threaten **Nadezhdin** and his team with prison if his supporters protest.

c. The fatal crash of a private jet. The Russians added a new method to the Kremlin's extensive assassination menu. The airplane carrying **Wagner chief Yevgeny Prigozhin** was shot from the sky on 23 Aug 2023, two months after he led a mutiny against Russia's top army brass.

d. **Poisoning.** Russian intelligence officials turned political poisonings into something of an art form. Below are some prominent cases of documented killings or attempted killings.

- Russia's dark methods first came to international attention during the case of **Alexander Litvinenko**, a Putin opponent who died of polonium-210 poisoning in London in 2006.

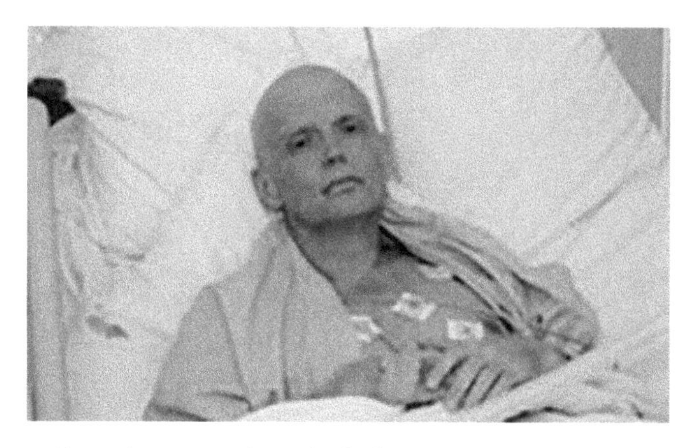

Alexander Litvinenko in his bed at Univ. College hospital, London before he died. Photograph: Getty

- In 2018, **Sergei Skripal**, a Russian military intelligence officer who had become a double agent for the UK, survived a poisoning with a nerve agent called ***Novichok*** in Salisbury, UK. Russian security services have also poisoned less prominent Russians, including the writers **Dmitry Bykov** and **Pyotr Verzilov**, who were evacuated to Germany for treatment shortly after falling ill and dying. Most recently, an investigative report by the independent news outlet ***the Insider*** alleged that three Russian journalists known for their anti-Kremlin stances might have been poisoned in foreign countries, including Germany and Georgia.

Russian opposition leader Alexei Navalny with his wife Yulia in Moscow in September 2013. (AP)

- But the most recent and horrible poisoning involves **Alexei Navalny,** the strongest opposition leader to Putin. In August 2020, **Navalny** fell ill on a flight from Siberia to Moscow. He was later flown to Germany for treatment, where doctors established that he had been poisoned with ***Novichok.*** Having survived the poisoning, **Navalny** returned to Russia and was jailed in Siberia to prevent his candidacy for Russian President. On 15 February 2024, the news reported that Navalny ***"died in prison today."*** Navalny's Chief of Staff and his mother corrected that report to ***"Putin killed Navalny today."*** Here are extracts from a 16 Feb 2024 Fox News article.

RUSSIAN MEDIA, PUTIN CRITIC NAVALNY DIES IN PRISON

Article from Fox News,
by Anders Hagstrom, 16Feb2024

Russian opposition leader Alexei Navalny's body was reportedly found with *"signs of bruising"* this weekend, while government officials told his mother on Saturday that Navalny died of *"sudden death syndrome."* Meanwhile, world leaders and Navalny's own spokesperson have declared that he was, in fact, murdered by Russian President Vladimir Putin's regime. Prison officials said Navalny, 47, fell unconscious and died shortly afterward on Friday. He had been serving a roughly 30-year sentence in a penal colony. ***"When Alexei's lawyer and mother arrived at the colony this morning, they were told that the cause of Navalny's death was sudden death syndrome,"*** Ivan Zhdanov, who directs Navalny's Anti-Corruption Foundation, announced on social media. ... Officials at the prison where Navalny died told his mother that his body could not be handed over until an investigation had been completed. They said his body was sent to a nearby morgue. An anonymous paramedic claiming to work for the morgue told independent news outlet Novaya Gazeta Europe that the bruising was consistent with a person being held down while suffering a seizure. ***"Usually the bodies of people who die in prison are taken straight to the Bureau of Forensic Medicine on Glazkova Street, but in this***

case it was taken to the clinical hospital for some reason," the anonymous paramedic told the outlet. Navalny had previously organized anti-government demonstrations and ran for office to advocate for reforms against what he called corruption in Russia. He was the victim of an alleged assassination attempt in 2020 when he suffered poisoning from a suspected Novichok nerve agent.

Here is a viewer's comment to the above article dated 16 February 2024 from **geopatriot: *"These Dems criticize the Russians for the same thing Biden has done to Trump and Conservatives in the USA since he became President, actually Biden is worse than Putin because we are supposed to live in freedom and democracy and free speech except if you are a conservative. Many Dems have questioned elections in the USA and no one on the left got charged. Everyone knows the 2020 election was rigged and the machines were hacked and states changed their voting laws before and during the elections in 2020. All over the world the leftist governments are destroying the lives of people and do not work for the people's best interests, but only for the politicians' interests or to make themselves richer. We are worse off than Russia."***

---

2. LEADERSHIP AND GOVERNANCE OF THE USA SINCE THE YEAR 2021. Let's begin this paragraph by informing our readers and the American people of the **TRUTH**, that **THE UNITED STATES HAS EXPERIENCED AN INSURRECTION, NOT on 6 January 2021** *(the peaceful demonstration that got out-of-hand in the Capitol)*, **but on 3 November 2020** *(the fraudulent election that allowed the takeover of the Executive and both houses of Congress by a consortium of Democrats and Marxist-influenced anarchists).* I must qualify the preceding too long sentence by reminding the reader of the 2nd part of ***"Goebbels Doctrine,"*** referenced earlier in this article, to ***"Accuse the other side of that for which you are guilty."*** **What the Democrats did on 3 Nov 2020, an insurrection using fake ballots to steal the election, is exactly what they accused the other side of doing, i.e. an insurrection by Republicans on 6 January 2021 to steal our government.**

a. The USA censoring and jailing members of the opposition can impact the 2024 election. Those who attempt to reveal the **TRUTH** about the fraudulent 3 Nov 2020 election are being prosecuted and punished by the ***"weaponized"*** Dept of Justice. Let's look at some of those prosecutions.

1) The case of former Trump advisor Peter Navarro. He served in the Trump administration as an Assistant to the President. He exposed the fraudulent Nov 3, 2020 election results which transformed a Trump victory as President on Nov 3, 2020 into a Joe Biden win 6 weeks after the election *(see adjacent graph).* Peter Navarro has been ordered to serve 4 months in prison. This penance is due to his claim of *"Executive Privilege"* for not testifying after receiving a subpoena from the Democratic Controlled House of Representatives in 2021.

Trump Red Tide Turns Blue

	GEORGIA	PENNSYLVANIA	MICHIGAN	WISCONSIN
Trump Lead Midnight 11/3	356,945	555,189	293,052	112,022
Biden "Lead" 12/15	11,779	81,660	154,188	20,682

FOX NEWS A LOOK INTO THE NAVARRO REPORT

2) Consider the fate of the demonstrators at the 6 January 2021 Capitol protest. More than 1,230 have been indicted for storming the U.S. Capitol building, with charges ranging from obstruction of an official proceeding to assault. Around 750 individuals have received criminal sentences, some of whom were not even in Washington D.C. on 6 January 2021.

3) What Democrats are doing to keep Donald Trump off the November 2024 presidential ballot. Mimicking the Russian corrupt legal system targeting political opponents, this prosecution is led by a weaponized Department of Justice using what is termed ***"Lawfare"*** (similar to the military term ***"Warfare"***) to jail a political opponent. **Donald Trump** has been prosecuted in 2023 on 91 federal and state charges, in four separate indictments, **that carry a maximum sentence of 717 years in prison if convicted.** Among the most egregious violations:

- President Donald Trump was indicted in May 2023, in a case brought by Manhattan District Attorney **Alvin Bragg**, on 34 charges revolving around $130,000 paid to adult film actress Stormy Daniels in 2016. The prosecution in a Manhattan Court Room, led by a corrupt Judge **Juan Merchan,** found him guilty of all 34 charges as **felonies** (vs. **misdemeanors).** The attempted sentencing by Judge Merchan meant to place Donald Trump in jail before the November 2024 election was delayed only by appeals.

 - He has been **fined over $650 million** on *"trumped up"* charges in an attempt to bankrupt his businesses.

 - The Secretary of States in Maine, Colorado and Illinois had also barred President Trump from the Year 2024 President ballots in their states prior to a Supreme Court 9-0 ruling forbidding this.

 - But the US Constitution provisions that separate the powers of the Executive, Legislative and Judicial systems prevailed. The Supreme Court issued a 1 July 2024 decision that Presidents are immune from criminal liability for official acts while in office. This ruling kept Donald Trump from imprisonment.

b. The USA Insurrection is fueled by an invasion of illegal immigrants and a corrupt voting process. Consider the following **TRUTHS** from media reports in 2024:

1) The invasions of the Ukraine and the USA. Both the Ukraine and the USA have been invaded since the Year 2021. The Russians invaded Ukraine in February 2022 and have experienced **over 460,000 MILITARY** killed or wounded in two years by the defending Ukrainian freedom fighters. The USA however, is not being invaded by a **MILITARY,** but by **9 to**

14 million unfortunate ILLEGAL IMMIGRANTS seeking refuge or a better life who cannot be eliminated in defense of the USA.

2) **The Biden administration is intentionally allowing illegal immigrants entry into the USA.** It is no secret that this is done in order to create more votes to allow the current occupiers of our nation to remain in power. Although our Constitution bars illegals from voting, the names of illegal immigrant are automatically added to voter rolls when they receive a driver license (most notably in the State of New York). These names are then available within programmable voting machines to cast ballots for the Democrats and Biden or Harris in the November 2024 election.

3) Musk says Biden opened *"border floodgates"* so Democrats can stay in power. Elon Musk exposed the Democrat party's process of adding illegal immigrants to the USA voting roles in a Feb 2024 news article. Musk claims that Biden wants to get as many illegal immigrants into the country so Democrats can create a permanent one-party state. The article exposes how **Non-Government Organizations** (NGOs), which are nonprofit organizations that operate independently of any government, and whose purpose is to address a social or political issue, channel over $1Billion in aid to illegal immigrants. The NGOs provide maps, spending money, flights to internal USA cities for some 340,000 illegals, contacts with cartel operatives to guide illegals to the USA border, and advice on what to tell border guards to expedite their *"catch and release"* to cities and states throughout the USA.

c. The deadly Oct. 7 2023 attack in southern Israel. Following the **Quran** verse to ***"kill the idolaters wherever you find them and take them prisoners,"*** the radical Islamist **Hamas** element of Palestine swarmed through their tunnels to massacre more than 1,200 Israelis and take 251 hostages from the kibbutzim of Israel. The Israeli Defense Forces have since entered Gaza to defend their citizens and eliminate the Hamas military threat to the survival of their Nation. This self-defense is necessary for the continued existence of an Israeli State. This **TRUTH** however, is not what our Ivy League Universities are teaching. Our universities are instead encouraging students to express the strongest exhibition of antisemitism since World War II. The attached photograph shows demonstrators supporting Hamas and the Palestinians rather than the Israeli nation. The protests have led to an array of different responses from universities. Many universities have called police and other law enforcement agencies on to campus. In the United States alone as of 30 April 2024, more than 2,000 students have been arrested. This is not limited to the United States. Both protests and the campus crackdowns have also spread to other parts of the world – from Canada to Australia - and in multiple European nations, including students at Oxford and Cambridge in the United Kingdom.

d. A ballot fraud study finds Trump *'Almost Certainly'* won in 2020. An Epoch Times News Article published Feb 13, 2024 reported that the massive expansion of mail-in voting—as well as the resultant fraud—almost certainly changed the outcome of the 2020 presidential election. The study was commissioned by the Heartland Institute and titled: ***"Who really won the 2020 election?"*** It concluded that had the 2020 election been conducted like every national election over the past two centuries, wherein the vast majority of voters cast ballots in-person rather than by mail, Donald Trump would have almost certainly been re-elected.

1) Expert shows how to tamper with Georgia voting machine in a security trial. Huddled around a voting machine in a federal courtroom, a small crowd watched as expert witness **Alex Halderman** demonstrated how someone could meddle with a Georgia election within seconds. **Alex Halderman**, a University of Michigan computer science professor, showed how a voting machine could be hacked during a 2018 hearing, and gave a similar demonstration in January 2024, in a trial to determine whether Georgia's voting system is vulnerable to manipulation or programming errors. **Halderman** flipped the winner in a theoretical election between President George Washington and Benedict Arnold, the Revolutionary War general who defected to the British. He rigged the machine to print out as many ballots as he wanted. All he needed was a pen to reach a button inside the touchscreen, a fake $10 voter card he had programmed, or a $100 USB device that he plugged into a cord connected to a printer to rewrite the touchscreen's code. ***"All of these things worry me — just how easy these machines would be to tamper with. It's so far from a secure system,"*** Halderman testified. ***"There are all kinds of politically motivated actors that would be eager to affect results."*** The 3 November 2020 fraudulent election took advantage of such faulty voting machines, and remotely located voting ballot drop boxes, to allow unelected leaders to take control of the USA government.

2) The weaponization of the USA justice system. There is more evidence of the corruption within the USA judicial system with the incredible $148 Million civil judgement against former New York City Mayor **Rudy Giuliani**. So what happened?

- **The ballet fraud of 4 November 2020 in Fulton County, GA.** The ***"vote count"*** was continuing at 2AM during the early morning after the 3 November election in Atlanta. This was after an election supervisor requested all witnesses to the ***"vote count"*** to vacate the State Farm Arena due to a bathroom leak somewhere in the building. A security video camera showed the wheeling of fake ballots from under a table at 2:30 AM, after all the witnesses were chased out of the Arena. The video camera also caught one of the ladies stuffing the same ballot into a voting machine 9-10 times. But this was the ***"normal way"*** to count votes in the State of Georgia. This clarification was offered by Deputy Secretary of State **Jordan Fuchs.** She explained this was the "***normal way"*** to count votes because, at times, the first pass of a ballot doesn't register in the voting machine!

- **The case of Rudy Giuliani's false claims of election fraud.** Here I must again remind the reader of the ***"Goebbels Doctrine"*** referenced earlier in this article. That ***"Doctrine"*** is to ***"Tell lies long enough to where people believe they are true;"*** and, to ***"Accuse the other side of that for which you are guilty."*** I've attached extracts from a biased liberal news media article below that discuss the Rudy Giuliani case. I have "hi-lited," used **bold print**, and **<u>underlined</u>** the controversial segments of the article to better expose the **LIES**. Here's the article:

GIULIANI APPEALS $148M FULTON DEFAMATION VERDICT

It's the latest twist in the case of his false claims of election fraud.

From the Atlanta Journal Constitution, written by Dave Wickert, 22 Feb 2024

Rudy Giuliani has appealed **a $148 million verdict against him** won by two former Fulton County election workers. **In December a federal jury in Washington, D.C.** *(my add: Why not in Georgia?)* **awarded Ruby Freeman and Shaye Moss the money because Giuliani falsely accused them of fraud in the 2020 election.**

The appeal is the latest twist in a case that began on election night 2020, when Freeman and Moss counted **absentee ballots** at State Farm Arena. A month later, Giuliani unveiled snippets of security footage from the counting to a Georgia Senate panel. He said the footage showed election workers illegally counting **fake ballots** they retrieved from beneath a table after election observers left for the night. **It did not. Investigators from the FBI, the GBI and the Secretary of State's Office reviewed the security footage and interviewed witnesses. They determined nothing improper happened — the footage showed normal ballot counting.** Giuliani also faces charges in the Fulton County election interference case for his alleged role in Trump's effort to overturn the election. **Several other people also have been charged in the case for their roles in trying to convince Freeman to confess to the false fraud allegations.**

---

e. The Republicans Are Mounting a Campaign To Oust Radical Marxists From Our Government. Republicans are attempting to take back our nation in the 2024 November election. There is hope for removal of the Marxist-influenced leaders of the USA from our government, but ***ONLY IF AMERICAN CITIZENS WITH VALIDATED ID'S VOTE***

IN SECURE VOTING BOOTHS USING NON-PROGRAMMABLE VOTING MACHINES. Let's end this warning memo to the readers of the book by sharing extracts from what two candidates will attempt to do if they are elected in November 2024.

1) An Email from Steve Garvey. I'm sharing extracts from an email received from Republican **Steve Garvey**, a candidate in the California Senate election against Democrat **Adam Schiff.** Garvey compares the abysmal happenings in 2024 to the horrific events that occurred in the 1960's-70's Vietnam War era.

Dear Friend, *If you opened this email because you remember my playing days with the Dodgers and the Padres, thank you. Having you and all of America's baseball fans cheering for me and the rest of the guys as we battled … the Yankees, well, as they say, "Those were the days." But this email isn't about baseball. In fact, Today, I'm asking you to help me defeat the radical Adam Schiff for a seat in the United States Senate. I'm asking you to help me start a Republican Comeback Rally that folks will be talking about for generations to come. Because when you think about it, those 'good-ol' days of the 1970s weren't as good as we tend to first remember. I'm running for the United States Senate because 2024 America is starting to look a lot like 1970s America. You remember what it was like:*

> *- Not only were gas prices sky high, Carter's rationing meant we could only buy gas on even or odd days depending on our license plate numbers.* ***Remember?***
>
> *- Eleven Israeli athletes were slaughtered at the Munich Olympics by terrorists.* ***Remember?***
>
> *- Fifty-two Americans were held hostage for 444 days by terrorists in Iran.* ***Remember??***

Democrat policies had brought America to its knees. And now, as Yogi Berra used to say, "It's déjà vu all over again."

> *- There's fear of walking down the street because of rampant crime, homelessness, and drug addiction.*

- The cost of living is exploding and for the first time causing more people to leave California.

- Joe Biden, Adam Schiff and the rest of the Democrats don't care one bit that Americans are having a hard time. I'd go even further to say they welcome the misery so they can keep folks down and dependent.

And I wouldn't blame you if you said, "Steve, I'm afraid America's best days are behind us."

But listen, here's something I also want you to remember. We Republicans pulled our country out of that 1970's Democratic malaise by electing Ronald Reagan. We put classic conservative values at the heart of everything we did. We can do that again. It starts by stunning Democrats with a Senate win in California. In March, I need to be one of the top 2 vote-getters to get to the November general election. Adam Schiff will probably take the #1 spot. And polls have me hot on his heels for the #2 spot. Once passed the primary, I know I can beat him in November. Why?

First... I've lived and worked in California for over 50 years. Voters here have had it with the Democrats like I've never seen before. They are hungry for change, and if you and I work together to reach voters...I know we can turn this historic opportunity into a Republican win.

Second... you know I'm not a career politician. But I do have the one thing a Republican needs to get elected in California...name recognition. I'm no Schwarzenegger and I'd certainly never dare compare myself to President Reagan. But California voters know me. Schiff and Democrats are shaking in their boots seeing how quickly I rose in the polls after entering the race. When we win here... we start the nationwide Republican Comeback Rally our country desperately needs. It all depends on you! Please join me. Because when we win in California, we're winning for all of America. Thank you and God Bless, ***Steve Garvey, Republican for United States Senate***

2) Trump vows to clear out Biden's 'communists who have weaponized government.

Article written by Eric Mack from
Newsmax, 10 February 2024

The two-tiered justice system under President Joe Biden will face a long overdue existential threat this November, former President Donald Trump vowed Friday night in his address to the National Rifle Association. ***"We will completely overhaul the corrupt Department of Justice to clear out all the communists who have weaponized government activities and gone against conservatives and gun owners. And we will replace them with relentless crime fighters on a mission to put the dangerous behind bars."*** Gone will be the days of soft enforcement of American laws, including the failure to enforce southern border and immigration law or the soft-on-crime policies in Democrat-run cities – all while the DOJ is weaponized against conservatives and even the religious – Trump vowed. ***"If you're a violent criminal today, if you kill people, if you slaughter people, if you mug people, nothing happens,"*** Trump said. ***"But if you're a religious person of a certain faith, you get persecuted. And I don't know what's going on with Catholics, but Catholics are being treated very badly."*** Trump warned that the 2020 presidential election featured nationwide lawlessness and Black Lives Matter and antifa rioting, weaponized by leftist agitators seeking to ***"defund the police"*** and defeat Trump to install a soft-on-crime Biden administration. ***"The day I'm inaugurated is the day that law and order, sanity, and justice will return back to the United States of America. On day one, we will seal the border and stop the invasion of America – we're being invaded just like it's a military invasion."***

f. Fraudulent elections have sustained Communist Rule in Venezuela throughout the 21st Century.

-Hugo Chávez was the Venezuelan politician who brought communist rule to Venezuela from 1999 until his death in 2013. He was succeeded by **Nicolas Maduro**, who has since retained the Presidency of Venezuela using fraudulent voting. Presidential elections were held in Venezuela on 28 July 2024 to choose a president for a six-year term beginning on 10 January 2025. While *"exit polls"* from voting booths showed former diplomat **Edmundo González Urrutia** receiving over 60% of the vote, **Nicolas Maduro** declared himself the winner with 51% of the vote. The government-controlled National Electoral Council falsified results to show a narrow Maduro victory on 29 July, but never provided the vote tallies to validate this election.

- **Edmundo González Urrutia** fled Venezuela after Maduro ordered his arrest for snubbing a probe into vote, and has sought exile in Spain. **Edmundo González** has joined the approximately **7 million Venezuelans** who have fled communist rule of their nation during the Maduro regime, with another **4 million to 7 million of Venezuela's 28 million population** forecasted to depart in the future if **Maduro** retains power.

g. The Year 2024 events in Venezuela demonstrated how important it is for citizens to have a voice in elections. We talked about the importance of citizens voting, and living in a Nation controlled by a constitution which ***"Creates a government that puts the power in the hands of the people."*** As Venezuelan dictator **Nicolás Maduro** continues his effort to steal a third Venezuelan presidential election, Florida Senators **Rick Scott** and **Marco Rubio** introduced legislation that would provide a maximum **$100 Million reward** for information leading to the arrest and conviction of Nicolás Maduro. The reward would be paid out by the federal government using seized assets already being withheld from Maduro. **Senator Rick Scott,** in a speech introducing the legislation, stated: *"The time has come for Venezuela to be liberated from the illegitimate regime of dictator* ***Nicolás Maduro****. For years, I have urged the Biden-Harris administration to use the full weight of the federal government to put an end to the Maduro regime, but it has refused and continued its failed appeasement that has only enriched and emboldened Maduro and his puppet masters in Cuba at the expense of the Venezuelan people. The Venezuelan people overwhelmingly voted for a new day of freedom and democracy on July 28 when they elected* ***Edmundo González*** *in an effort led by opposition leader* ***María Corina Machado****. It's clear Maduro will not step down on his own, and I urge my colleagues to support this bill to rid Venezuela and the world of Maduro's oppression and make way for President-elect González to bring democracy, freedom and opportunity back to Venezuela."*

3. THE LEADERS I DISCOVERED IN GERMANY. I was fortunate enough to work and live in Germany between 1971-1986. During my time there, I learned about two influentials leaders that I must share with you. They are the German World War II **Field Marshall Erwin Rommel**, and the American Cold War hero **General Bill Livsey**, under whom I served for 4 years from 1978-82. Let me tell you about them.

a. Field Marshall Erwin Rommel. The ***"Desert Fox"*** was best known for his military prowess as the Commander of the Afrika Korps in Tunisia, and for being in charge of the Nazi Normandy Beach defenses before the 6 June 1944 Allied D-Day invasion of France. The ***International Churchill Society*** labeled Erwin Rommel ***'a thoroughly decent man'*** in recognition of Rommel as one of Nazi Germany's most prolific commanders, and to commemorate his tendency to ignore many of Hitler's most horrible orders. Hitler ordered the death of Field Marshall Rommel after a failed assassination attempt on Hitler's life that Rommel was aware of, but did not participate in. But because Rommel was extremely popular with the German folk, Hitler sent two generals to his home with ***poison*** for Rommel to take and commit suicide. **Field Marshall Erwin Rommel** was the father of **Manfred Rommel,** the mayor of **Stuttgart Germany** during the 1980s and who had significant involvement with US Army's VII Corps during the European Cold War. Manfred Rommel's interaction with his father during WWII is below.

- **The Forced Suicide of Field Marshall Rommel, 1944.** The difficult decision that *Joseph Goebbels* made in May 1945, about the fate and forced suicide of his wife and five children in a Berlin bunker, was also a decision faced by ***Field Marshall Erwin Rommel*** earlier in the war, in October 1944. *(Note: I have a closer connection to the Rommel family because I knew the son, Manfred Rommel, the Mayor of Stuttgart, when I worked for the US Army in the 1980s in Germany. My mentor and boss at that time, the VII Corps Commander Lieutenant General Bill Livsey, had a close association with – no – more than that - a close friendship with - Manfred Rommel).* LTG Bill Livsey and Mayor Manfred Rommel had many contacts with each other, and indeed became close lifetime friends. How Manfred Rommel survived World War II however, is best described in his own words in the story below and in the three photos:

Field Marshall Erwin Rommel with the Afrika Korps in 1941

Manfred Rommel at age 15 with his mother and Field Marshall Erwin Rommel in 1944

And Manfred Rommel as the Mayor of Stuttgart in the 1980s

- Hitler Decided that Field Marshall Rommel must die. For a time, Erwin Rommel was Hitler's favorite general. Gaining prominence in 1940 as a commander of a panzer division that smashed the French defenses, Rommel went on to command the Afrika Korps where his tactical genius, ability to inspire his troops and make the best of limited resources, prompted Hitler to elevate him to the rank of Field Marshall. In 1943, Hitler placed Rommel in command of fortifying the *"Atlantic Wall"* along the coast of France - defenses intended to repel the inevitable D-day invasion of Europe by the Allies. By the beginning of 1943, Rommel's faith in Germany's ability to win the war was crumbling, as was his estimation of Hitler. Touring

Germany, Rommel was appalled at the devastation of the Allied bombing raids and the erosion of the peoples' morale. He also learned for the first time of the death camps, slave labor, the extermination of the Jews and the other atrocities of the Nazi regime. Rommel became convinced that victory for Germany was a lost cause and that prolonging the war would lead only to his homeland's devastation. He came in contact with members of a growing conspiracy dedicated to ousting Hitler and establishing a separate peace with the western allies. On July 17, 1944, British aircraft strafed Rommel's staff car, severely wounding the Field Marshall. He was taken to a hospital and then to his home in Germany to convalesce. Three days later, an assassin's bomb nearly killed Hitler during a strategy meeting at his headquarters in East Prussia. In the gory reprisals that followed, some suspects implicated Rommel in the plot. Although he may not have been aware of the attempt on Hitler's life, his *"defeatist"* attitude was enough to warrant Hitler's wrath. The problem for Hitler was how to eliminate Germany's most popular general without revealing to the German people that he had ordered his death. The solution was to force Rommel to commit suicide and announce that his death was due to his battle wounds.

- **The day of death for a German Hero**. Rommel's son, Manfred, was 15 years old and served as part of an antiaircraft crew near his home. On **October 14th, 1944** Manfred was given leave to return to his home where his father continued to convalesce. **The family was aware that Rommel was under suspicion, and that his chief of staff and his commanding officer had both been executed.**

Manfred's account begins as he enters his home and finds his father at breakfast: *"...I arrived at Herrlingen at 7:00 a.m. My father was at breakfast. A cup was quickly brought for me and we breakfasted together, afterwards taking a stroll in the garden.* ***'At twelve o'clock today two Generals are coming to discuss my future employment,'*** my father started the conversation. ***'So today will decide what is planned for me; whether a People's Court or a new command in the East.' 'Would you accept such a command,'*** *I asked. He took me by the arm, and replied:* ***'My dear boy, our enemy in the East is so terrible that every other consideration has to give way before it. If he succeeds in overrunning***

Europe, even only temporarily, it will be the end of everything which has made life appear worth living. Of course I would go.'

Shortly before twelve o'clock, my father went to his room on the first floor and changed from the brown civilian jacket which he usually wore over riding-breeches, to his Africa tunic, which was his favorite uniform on account of its open collar. At about twelve o'clock a dark-green car with a Berlin number stopped in front of our garden gate. The only men in the house apart from my father, were Captain Aldinger [Rommel's aide], a badly wounded war-veteran corporal and myself. Two generals - ***Burgdorf,*** *a powerful florid man, and* ***Maisel****, small and slender - alighted from the car and entered the house. They were respectful and courteous and asked my father's permission to speak to him alone. Aldinger and I left the room.* ***'So they are not going to arrest him,'*** *I thought with relief, as I went upstairs to find myself a book. A few minutes later I heard my father come upstairs and go into my mother's room. Anxious to know what was afoot, I got up and followed him. He was standing in the middle of the room, his face pale.* ***'Come outside with me,'*** *he said in a tight voice. We went into my room.* ***'I have just had to tell your mother,'*** *he began slowly,* ***'that I shall be dead in a quarter of an hour.'***

He was calm as he continued: ***'To die by the hand of one's own people is hard. But the house is surrounded and Hitler is charging me with high treason.' 'In view of my services in Africa,'*** *he quoted sarcastically,* ***'I am to have the chance of dying by poison. The two generals have brought it with them. It's fatal in three seconds. If I accept, none of the usual steps will be taken against my family, that is against you. They will also leave my staff alone.' "Do you believe it?"*** *I interrupted.* ***'Yes,'*** *he replied.* ***'I believe it. It is very much in their interest to see that the affair does not come out into the open. By the way, I have been charged to put you under a promise of the strictest silence. If a single word of this comes out, they will no longer feel themselves bound by the agreement.'*** *I tried again.* ***"Can't we defend ourselves."*** *He cut me off short.* ***'There's no point,'*** *he said.* ***'It's better for one to die than for all of us to be killed in a shooting affray. Anyway, we've practically no ammunition.'*** *We briefly took leave of each other.* ***'Call Aldinger, please,'*** *he said.*

Aldinger had meanwhile been engaged in conversation by the General's escort to keep him away from my father. At my call, he came running upstairs. He, too, was struck cold when he heard what was happening. My father now spoke more quickly. He again said how useless it was to attempt to defend ourselves. ***'It's all been prepared to the last detail. I'm to be given a state funeral. I have asked that it should take place in Ulm*** *[a town near Rommel's home].* ***In a quarter of an hour, you, Aldinger, will receive a telephone call from the Wagnerschule reserve hospital in Ulm to say that I've had a brain seizure on the way to a conference.'*** *He looked at his watch.* ***'I must go, they've only given me ten minutes.'***

He quickly took leave of us again. Then we went downstairs together. We helped my father into his leather coat. Suddenly he pulled out his wallet. ***'There's still 150 marks in there,'*** *he said.* ***'Shall I take the money with me?' "That doesn't matter now, Herr Field Marshal,"*** *said Aldinger. My father put his wallet carefully back in his pocket. As he went into the hall, his little dachshund which he had been given as a puppy a few months before in France, jumped up at him with a whine of joy.* ***'Shut the dog in the study, Manfred,'*** *he said, and waited in the hall with Aldinger while I removed the excited dog and pushed it through the study door. Then we walked out of the house together.*

The two generals were standing at the garden gate. We walked slowly down the path, the crunch of the gravel sounding unusually loud. As we approached the generals they raised their right hands in salute. ***'Herr Field Marshal,'*** *Burgdorf said shortly and stood aside for my father to pass through the gate. A knot of villagers stood outside the drive. The car stood ready. The S.S. driver swung the door open and stood to attention. My father pushed his Marshal's baton under his left arm, and with his face calm, gave Aldinger and me his hand once more before getting in the car. The two generals climbed quickly into their seats and the doors were slammed. My father did not turn again as the car drove quickly off up the hill and disappeared round a bend in the road. When it had gone Aldinger and I turned and walked silently back to the house.*

Twenty minutes later the telephone rang. Aldinger lifted the receiver and my father's death was duly reported. ***"It was not then entirely clear, what had happened to him after he left us. Later we learned that the car had halted a few hundred yards up the hill from our house in an open space at the edge of the wood. Gestapo men, who had appeared in force from Berlin that morning, were watching the area***

with instructions to shoot my father down and storm the house if he offered resistance. Maisel and the driver got out of the car, leaving my father and Burgdorf inside. When the driver was permitted to return ten minutes or so later, he saw my father sunk forward with his cap off and the marshal's baton fallen from his hand."*(Ref:Hart, B.H.Liddell, The Rommel Papers(1953); Roger Manvell,Heinrich Fraenkel, The Men Who Tried to Kill Hitler 1964).*

b. General Bill J. Livsey. General MacArthur once mentioned in a West Point speech that ***"old soldiers never die, they just fade away."*** If only that could have applied to General Livsey. He was commissioned into the Army from North Georgia University in Dahlonega, GA and served in the Korean War in 1953. He was my Commanding General in Germany between 1978-1983. He ended his career where he started it - in Korea - as Commander of all allied forces in the region. He might have been the leader of the US military during the 1991 Gulf War, had he not ended his military career in 1987. GEN Livsey had returned to Georgia, his home state, in retirement. He had a Georgia highway named after him near his retirement home in Fayetteville GA. He also had an athletic field named in his honor at the North Georgia military school that he attended. But the last 3 years of his life had not been kind to him. He lost his wife of 60 years in 2013, and his son, Bill Livsey III, died at age 60 in 2014. At the age of 84 on 15 August 2015, he placed a telephone order for a Chinese food delivery to his home. The rest of this story is taken from the August 19th and August 20th news. There are two versions.

1) General Livsey is arrested and thrown in jail in 2015. I picked up the newspaper on 19 August 2015 and, to my great dismay, found that General Livsey was in a Fayette County jail. I'm attaching three photographs of General Livsey below, followed by two text boxes with the newspaper story.

Photo of *"Livsey's Famous Smile"* in a 1979 newspaper in Germany.

Photo of normal General Livsey (left) and the mug shot that appeared in the Atlanta news and Wikipedia after his arrest.

---

(1) Man accused of not paying for food, assaulting driver. *(from the **Atlanta Journal Constitution**).* A retired four-star general was out on bond Tuesday after being taken to the Fayette County jail over the weekend for allegedly ordering Chinese food without paying for it and then assaulting a delivery driver.

"It was the worst thing that happened to me in all of my life," William J. Livsey told The Atlanta Journal-Constitution, recalling the ***"10 cops here for one 84-year-old man"*** at his Fayetteville home Saturday evening. In an emailed statement to the AJC, **Fayetteville police Chief Scott Pitts** said that after his order from the Royal Chef restaurant arrived at his home, Livsey tried to pay the driver with a debit card that was declined. When Livsey offered to pay with a check instead, the driver told him checks were not accepted by the restaurant and he would have to take the food back, the police chief said. That is when Livsey allegedly grabbed the driver's throat and facial hair, pushed him and pinned him against a refrigerator in his kitchen. During the assault, police said, two people in the home took the food, placed it on a counter and began eating it. The driver was ultimately released and reported the incident to police, the chief said. Officers went to Livsey's home in the 200 block of Carriage Chase. Police said he told them he ordered the food and consumed some of it without paying for it. He also said the delivery driver pushed him when his debit card was rejected, Pitts said. As officers tried to handcuff him, Livsey resisted, according to the police chief. The struggle created a small laceration on Livsey's arm. Fayette County EMS was called to the scene to treat the injury and police tried to handcuff Livsey again. The police chief said Livsey tried ***"to punch one of the officers and kick another one all while making threatening and disparaging remarks."*** *In an interview with the AJC, the retired general spoke with emotion over what he called his mistreatment by authorities.* ***"It's the first time in my life I'm ashamed to be an American,"*** Livsey said. ***"They took me away without my shoes, glasses or medicine."*** He added, ***"I fought for this country so hard, and I've tried to do good all my life."*** Livsey was taken to the Fayette County jail on charges of robbery, misdemeanor obstruction, theft of services, simple assault and terroristic threats. The retired general said there were several guests at his house at the time of the incident. He said he sent his assistant to the restaurant to pay for the food and give the driver a tip. Livsey also said Royal Chef wanted to drop the incident but the Fayetteville police ***"made a spectacle of it and a spectacle of me."*** Livsey said his bond was set at $12,000 but he said ***"I didn't have to pay that. The judge released me on my own recognizance."***

(2) Eyewitness accounts differ in Gen. Livsey arrest Fayetteville (*from the Fayette County Register*).

Eyewitness says police still have not asked what he and other witnesses saw; victim tried to withdraw complaint, but police refused. Cops say retired 4-star general choked delivery driver, resisted arrest; eyewitness says cops over-reacted, dispute didn't happen the way warrants allege. **William "Bill" Livsey,** 84, of Fayetteville, a retired four-star general and Silver Star recipient for heroism, ordered home delivery for himself and three other companions from a Chinese restaurant just before 7 p.m. Aug. 15. Within a couple of hours that Saturday night, the highly decorated retired officer was handcuffed with bloody arms inside a Fayetteville police unit on his way to be booked into jail on charges including theft of services, two counts of obstruction of officers, simple assault, terroristic threats and acts, as well as a felony charge of robbery, per the magistrate court warrants and police reports. Livsey's bail bond was set at $12,000. Following questions from The Citizen, Police Chief **Scott Pitts**, City Manager **Ray Gibson** and Mayor **Greg Clifton** have released their side of the story. The general's personal caregiver and driver, **Tim Bedgood** of Sharpsburg, gives a sharply different version of events. Bedgood charges that multiple officers ***("seven cop cars and nine officers")*** mishandled the complaint, including handcuffing the 84-year-old so tightly his wrists bled. The official version ***"is not accurately portrayed,"*** Bedgood said, adding that he and two women were in the home from the time the call for takeout was made until the takeout delivery driver left the home. Bedgood said he left to pay the food bill in person at the restaurant, and when he returned, police in force had Livsey in cuffs outside with individual police units stationed at several intersections in the neighborhood. Not one of the eyewitnesses was interviewed the night of incident about what they saw, Bedgood said. By Tuesday afternoon, Bedgood said, he still had not been asked by police for his version of events. He said he asked the police captain as officers were taking Livsey away, did they know who they had in custody. ***"We know exactly who he is; we know he had a highway named after him,"*** the captain responded to Bedgood, he said Tuesday. **Livsey was released Monday on bond after spending two nights in jail.**

The dispute between Gen. Livsey, a widower who lost his wife of 60 years in July 2013, and the restaurant delivery driver involved payment of **$80.60** for the takeout order, according to warrants filed by police. The paperwork say the general's debit card was turned down after being called in by the driver, **Ryan Irvin**. The Royal Chef Chinese restaurant refused to take a personal check, the warrants allege. What happened then, the warrants allege, was a physical dispute over payment of the bill or return of the food. Livsey is alleged to have assaulted the delivery driver by placing his left hand around the driver's neck and pushing him against the refrigerator, warrants said. ***(Note: this part of the report from the Fayette County Register is with my added "hi-lites" or "italics.")*** **Bedgood** - who was present and witnessed the whole thing - has a different version of events. He said the general had misplaced his cash and gave the delivery driver an expired debit card. When Livsey offered a check, Irvin refused and reached to retrieve the bags of food being carried in by a woman. **At that point, Bedgood said, Gen. Livsey stepped between Irvin and the woman and *"grabbed Ryan by the arm, saying 'Talk to me, talk to me.'"*** Irvin left the Livsey residence without either payment or the food, the warrants allege. **The general's driver, Bedgood, said that he himself paid for the food within 20 minutes of the initial event. He also says that Irvin had tried to withdraw his complaint, allegedly saying that the situation was completely overblown. An interview with Irvin verified that point. Irvin said Tuesday night he had told a Fayetteville police captain that he wanted to drop the charges but was told that it was not possible. Bedgood said that he talked with Irvin, who allegedly told Bedgood that Irvin had *"a shouting match with a captain"* about the charge that the general had gripped his neck. Bedgood said that Irvin told the captain that the general had never touched his neck, only his arm.**

---

2) A rendezvous with General Bill Livsey. You may recall that we began this book discussing my visit to the Salisbury Cathedral in Great Britain on 30 November 2019. If not, let me recount it for you. It was in Salisbury where I discovered that Russia had reinitiated the 1945-1991 "***Cold War***" as evidenced by the attempted assassination of former Russian military officer and United Kingdom Intelligence Services double agent **Sergei Skripal** and his daughter **Yulia.** I wanted to do my small part to help restore the USA as ***"One Nation Under God"*** governed by the ***"Rule of Law"*** and a ***"constitution."*** I needed help. I therefore entered the museum section of the Salisbury Cathedral seeking a military leader and someone who could show me how to write! As an author of a fiction book, I took advantage of imagination and created a scene inside the museum section which would allow me to beckon General Bill Livsey to help me. Here's that fabricated story.

- I'm inside the museum section of the Salisbury Cathedral standing in front of the Magna Carta. I come with some of my grand-daughter Zuzu's ***Magic Dust.*** That ***"Magic Dust"*** is what she uses to become invisible, or move to another place in her home, to avoid unpleasant things - like when her parents tell her it's bedtime and she wants to stay up a bit longer. Zuzu provided me access to her ***"Magic Dust"*** whenever I needed it to contact anyone from history in writing this book. That's how I now can contact General Bill Livsey and continue this story.

- I pull out Zuzu's ***Magic Dust*** and sprinkle it over the Magna Carta casing. **Something is happening!** A cloud appears. There is a lot of huffing and puffing noises, hopefully not loud enough to attract the attention of the Salisbury Cathedral guides standing up the corridor outside the museum. And then **a figure** slowly appears – someone **I recognize** and **most admire** – someone I REALLY want to see and speak to:

"Hello General Bill Livsey! Welcome SIR to Great Britain!!!

The arrival of General Bill Livsey. It was great to once again be with General Bill Livsey. We had some ***catching up*** to do.

George: *Welcome to Salisbury Cathedral in Great Britain Sir! It's good to see you!*

General Livsey: *Where am I? Did you say Salisbury and Great Britain? What am I doing here, and how did I get here?*

George: *I'm not sure how, but I was in need of great assistance. And with the help of Salisbury Cathedral and the Magna Carta from the Year 1215, and Granddaughter Zuzu's Magic Dust, you were able to come here. Do you remember me?*

General Livsey: *Of course I remember you from Germany. It was during the early 1980's while we were both at VII Corps in Stuttgart. It's good to see you again George. And now please explain* ***"What's goin' on?"***

George: *Well Sir, the World is again in trouble. A lot has happened since your death in 2016. A billionaire real estate mogul and television reality star named* ***Donald Trump*** *upset* ***Hillary Clinton*** *and won the Presidential Election in November 2016. The opposition never accepted that election. It has been doing everything to destroy him since the day he was elected. And radical Islamic worldwide attacks are continuing. As a result, both the United States and the United Kingdom are engaged in a* ***two-front*** *war against* ***secular-Socialism*** *and* ***radical Islam****. To make matters even worse, the* ***"Cold War"*** *that you helped end when you were VII Corps Commanding General in Germany just* ***"resurfaced."*** *Thus we have a scenario that is threatening the continued existence of Western culture and a religion-based way of life as we know it. I therefore decided to try to do something about it. I'm calling all of this the* ***"4th War"*** *of my lifetime. I'm entering the fight. I'm also trying to write a book about it, and I'm failing. That's why I called on you SIR. The World and I once again need your help!*

General Livsey: *That's a lot of* ***"catching up"*** *in a short paragraph. But George, I'm dead. I've been dead since 2016. I'm not really here. I'm just a figment of your imagination. I am not real. You say you're writing a book and that has something to do with what you think you see. Anybody who reads this book will know that you made me up.*

George: *Actually Sir, you are not DEAD. You might not realize it, but you influenced a lot of events and a lot of people, especially me, during your stay* *on Earth. So in a manner of speaking, your* ***spirit*** *and* ***deeds*** *that impacted those who came in contact with you* ***"live on."***

General Livsey: *Thank you for the compliment George, but I'm still dead. But – (pause) - even if this* ***spirit*** *of Bill Livsey that you think and talk about was able to re-surface, what would you want from me?*

George: *That's hard to explain, but I'll try. First and foremost, Sir, you are not DEAD, because you really do live on and continue your existence by the impact you have had ON EVERYONE YOU CAME IN CONTACT WITH. And I need you now to help me. I'm failing in writing a book. I'm not communicating. I'm putting people to sleep trying to follow what I'm saying. I'm making it more complicated than it is. And besides all that and most important, I'm talking about a* ***4th War*** *that I'm about to enter as an 83-year-old. I need someone brilliant to help me – someone with military experience – someone who knows how to write and communicate – and that's you!*

General Livsey: *Well George. I'm still not quite sure what I can do to help you, or whether you made the* ***right decision*** *in nominating me for this honor. To be honest – I don't remember much from the last year of my life. Also, I'm not sure that whatever* ***"skills"*** *that might have previously been honed into me by the wonderful experience of life on Earth would even apply to the world of today.*

George: *Actually Sir, I'm very sure you're the right one to help me. I did a lot of research for this book to make sure you were the correct spirit to guide me to the finish. If we were using political terms, you've been thoroughly* ***"vetted,"*** *where* ***"vetted"*** *means* ***"having put someone or something through an extremely careful examination."***

General Livsey: *I know what you're doing. You recall, from your "****vetting"*** *of me, that I had psychology graduate training at Vanderbilt University and taught at West Point. So if you're trying to* ***psych*** *me into relaxing and agreeing to help you (after a slight pause)- well - OK - it worked. I'll help you with the military mentor thing and writing, as you call it, your* ***Damn Book.***

I'm still not sure what I've got into, or how I got into this commitment to help you. Please tell me more.

George: *The existentialism of the American Way of Life is being threatened. We have to assure our Constitution and Bill of Rights and the Rule of Law are restored in the USA if we are to have any chance of surviving. Too many conservative leaders in our nation are charged with treason or other crimes and are being prosecuted. That happened to you back in the Year 2015. I originally left your story out of the book because it sullied your legacy. What happened to you in 2015 is happening now to many who, during your lifetime, might have been considered heroes.*

General Livsey: *The last days of my life on Earth were kinda foggy. I don't remember much of that last year before I died. I just know I had a really bad experience that shook my faith in the United States. Yes I had similar thoughts about defending the country and the values it stands for back then, as you do now. But I can't say my thoughts to "get back into it" had anything to do with the Chinese food incident.*

George *(uncontrollably and inexplicably laughing)*: *I'm sorry Sir – I just can't help it! I just reviewed the news accounts of your arrest. Be honest with me Sir. The police only had five or six charges against you as you were (quoting from the newspaper)* ***"to be booked into jail on charges including theft of services, two counts of obstruction of officers, simple assault, terroristic threats and acts, as well as a felony charge of robbery."*** *Your aide said it was 9 cops that came and got you. You said 10 cops.* ***"How could you let just 9 or 10 cops on only 5 or 6 charges get the best of you?"***

General Livsey: ***"Shit George – I just got old – like 84 years old!"*** *But your story-telling and use of* ***"humor"*** *succeeded. You got that* ***"bullshit"*** *story out of the way, and more importantly, you got both of us to laugh about it. So now what do you want from me?*

George: *I need your help organizing the book and getting the message across about a very real existential threat to our way of life in our Nation. The November 2024 elections will be critical if we are to restore governance by leaders elected by US citizens rather than by fake ballots or* ***"harvested votes."*** *(Note:* ***"harvested votes"*** *is a legal process, originated in California,* *that allows someone other than a legal voter to cast ballots months before and up to 10 days after the election polls close). I was invited to write a Chapter for a* ***"Leaders Anthology"*** *book for Best Seller Publishing. It was rejected, but my Client Manager Bob Harpole, a former minister, encouraged me to still do a book submittal about Leaders. This is it. And I can't complete the book without nominating you as the leader who has most influenced by life, and who has save-guarded the values of the United States during your 35-year military career.*

George continues: *And you sir, are the final part of this book. I am nominating you to be one of the two leaders I discovered while I worked and lived in Germany between 1971-1986. I will send the final version of this book to a publishing agent, and hope they can publish it before the November 2024 election. It's my way of encouraging American citizens to vote and choose our national leaders without the use of programmable voting machines or fake ballots. It's the only way that we might be able to restore the United States as a Nation under God governed by a constitution, and to have the USA resume its role as the guardian of peace in the world.*

3) A little more about General Bill Livsey.

- The current nuclear threat from North Korea is due in part to the United States not being able to successfully finish the Korean War. General Bill Livsey did his part in attempting to solve the leftover mess from that War. He earned a Silver Star as an infantry combat platoon leader in 1953, and ended his military career 34 years later as a four-star general commanding both the United States and United Nation Forces in South Korea from 1984 to 1987.

- General Livsey is extremely intelligent. He probably had a photographic memory. He used short, clear sentences when he spoke, and came across as a simple *"good-old-boy"* when addressing his troops. He graduated first in his class at the US Army Command and General Staff College. He had a Master's Degree in Psychology from Vanderbilt University. He taught at the US Military Academy in West Point during his career. His academic legacy might be summarized by the teaching style General Livsey practiced during his military career to ***"tell 'um what you're gonna tell 'um,"*** then ***"tell 'um,"*** and end with ***"tell 'um what you told 'um."***

- I had the honor of serving under his command in Germany. We loved him. The Germans loved him. Allow me to share some stories about him to introduce you to the General William Livsey I know, and to illustrate the influence he had on both my wife and myself.

(a) The Open House. I was a civilian serving in Baumholder Germany in 1979 when the Community had an *"open house,"* with *"display booths"* in an open field to exhibit the available community services. I was in the Engineer booth when an elderly man in civilian clothing approached the different booths. I immediately recognized him as the not-in-uniform Commander of the 8th Infantry Division. He was never an ordinary Commander. He was likeable, personable, and a motivational type of leader. He spoke to everyone and anyone. So, of course I left my booth and joined MG Livsey. He approached a Civilian Personnel booth, where a representative was presenting *"Job Fair"* employment information. At the end of her presentation, this special elderly gentleman asked ***"Tell me, do you think you might be able to find me a job?"*** The young lady looked at MG Livsey for a few moments, then advised him cautiously ***"I'm sorry sir, but I'm afraid you are too old to get a job."*** So the Commander of the 8th Infantry Division couldn't get a shot at applying for work! We all had a good laugh, and especially the young lady, when she found out that the man who asked about work was the boss of the entire US military communities in both Bad Kreuznach and Baumholder!

(b) His Photographic Memory. I was reassigned to VII Corps and moved with my family to Stuttgart, Germany in December 1981. Bill Livsey had pinned on a third star by then and was now the Commanding General of VII Corps. He had a photographic memory. He remembered the names of everyone in his Korea 40-man platoon from 1953, and would reference members by name in his stories. That impacted me. I remembered less than half of my platoon members from my 1967-68 year in Vietnam.

(c) Swagger Sticks. Lieutenant General Livsey had a *"swagger stick"* that he carried with him everywhere. So let's talk a bit more about *"swagger sticks"* before proceeding.

- In ancient Rome, a swagger stick was a short stick or riding crop usually carried by a uniformed person as a symbol of authority. Its use by Roman centurions was an emblem of office.

- In the British Army, officers of infantry regiments carried swagger sticks when on duty. Cavalry officers would carry a riding crop rather than swagger stick in deference to mounted traditions.

- In the United States, swagger sticks were also in vogue in the United States military. General George S. Patton carried a swagger stick throughout World War II. His contained a concealed blade, similar to a Victorian gentleman's sword cane.

- In WWII Germany, Field Marshall Erwin Rommel carried a swagger stick. He had his *"baton"* with him when he was forced to take poison and commit suicide *(reference the preceding story about Rommel's forced suicide).*

- And General William J. Livsey, Commanding General of the Eighth United States Army in South Korea from 1984-87, publicly carried a swagger stick carved from wood collected at the Korean Demilitarized Zone. He's even mentioned in Wikipedia as part of the definition of swagger sticks.

- I remember attending a VII Corps social event with my dear wife Suava at Kelley Barracks Stuttgart in 1982. Yes, Lieutenant General Livsey had that *"swagger stick"* with him when he arrived. LTG Livsey approached us and began talking to us. Suava, in her most charming, direct and wonderful way, asked him ***"What is that stick for?"*** With his famous smile, he answered her ***"This is what I use to chase away beautiful women like you!"***

(d) His "Next Assignment" after VII Corps. It was the summer of 1983, and time for the Army to change the VII Corps Commander. There was a relatively long period with no word from Washington on General Livsey's next assignment. It was visibly wearing on him. The VII Corps staff had a continuing high regard for him, and wished for him to continue an active military career vs. a forced retirement. I recall being in his office during the wait period for his next assignment, and asking him about it. He explained to me that 3-star generals serve at the pleasure of the President of the United States, or retired. But the long wait ended well. He was reassigned from July 1983 until April 1984 to Fort McPherson in Atlanta, where he served as the Deputy Commander of the US Army Forces Command as well as the Commanding General, Third US Army. It was from here that the President of the United States appointed him a four-star general and assigned him to be the Commanding General of the 30,000 combined US and United Nation forces in South Korea from 1984 until his retirement in 1987.

4) What others say about him. Below are comments from two military members who served with General Bill Livsey.

(a) James Clapper, the Director of National Intelligence (DNI) for President Obama from 2010 through 2017. James Clapper had extensive experience in the intelligence business as a military general and with US spy agencies. He served under our **General Bill Livsey** as the G2 Intelligence Chief in Korea in 1986. He later served as the Director of the Defense Intelligence Agency (DIA) under President George H. W. Bush in 1991. President Obama appointed Clapper to the DNI position in 2010, a job Clapper held until the end of President Obama's term of office in January 2017. James Clapper was unfortunately involved in the 5 January 2017 meeting, set-up by President Obama's outgoing US intelligence and law enforcement agencies, in what would become the origin of the first ***"coups de etat"*** attempt to oust a sitting US President with the false ***"Trump-Russia Collusion Investigation."*** In his memoirs, Clapper recalls his time as a brigadier general serving in South Korea, where he got a good look at the paranoid, trigger-happy Hermit Kingdom. He referenced his assignment in Korea as the Intelligence Officer serving under **General Bill Livsey** in his book titled ***"Facts and Fears: Hard Truths from a Life in Intelligence."*** Let me share some excerpts from when James Clapper mentioned **General Bill Livsey** in his memoirs ***"Kim Jong Un is a God in North Korea"***

> *- My "big boss," Commander of US Forces Korea, Army four-star general Bill Livsey, had been a lieutenant platoon leader with the 3rd Infantry Division during the Korean War and dug in on the front line when the armistice took effect on July 27, 1953. He knew his business and suffered no fools. He was salty, and in the tradition of General George Patton,*

excelled at colorful profanity when the occasion called for it. On day one, he made it very clear that the Korean War had never formally ended, the 1953 armistice was just a cease-fire agreement, and North Korea could, and would, invade the South if given the opportunity.

- From that premise, he gave me his very clear expectations for intelligence. He demanded forty-eight hours of warning ahead of a North Korean attack to give him time to activate the operations plan for the defense of the peninsula and to evacuate all US dependents in South Korea. And because taking those irrevocable actions would have huge diplomatic consequences for the United States and major political implications for the ROK, Livsey required a forty-eight-hour "unambiguous" warning—we had to know for certain that an attack was imminent, and not a bluff or a feint. General Livsey was not one for subtle nuance.

(b) A newspaper obituary titled *"A Soldier's Soldier, recently gone but not forgotten"* dated 2 Jul 2016. This news article was written By **Robert B. Simpson**, a 28-year Infantry veteran who retired as a colonel at Ft Benning, and is the author of ***"Through the Dark Waters: Searching for Hope and Courage."***

*- **General William J. Livsey** died two weeks ago. I had just a few days before being regaled by a friend with Livsey stories. It was easy to remember stories about him, because he was a complex, often entertaining person. A product of North Georgia, both the region and the college, he was commissioned in the Infantry in 1953 and served as a platoon leader during the latter days of the Korean War.*

*- I'd never heard of the man when I arrived at the 4th Infantry Division's base camp at Dragon Mountain, near Pleiku, South Vietnam. I was told to report to Lieutenant Colonel Livsey, division G3, to be interviewed for possible assignment as his operations officer. The interview was brief. **"You've been an operations officer at those levels and have been shot at before and have the Combat Infantryman's Badge,"** he said. **"You don't need to go back out in the boondocks all over again. You can do more good here."***

- My first day on the job, Colonel Livsey chewed me out loudly over some small matter I no longer recall. I do recall that the reprimand was unfair and that I seethed as I stood there and took it. I feared that my anger would show on my face, for I am not good at hiding such feelings. The next day he jumped on me again, but that time instead of anger I suddenly found the whole thing funny. And that time, I really couldn't hide my feelings. As he chewed, I began to grin, sliding gradually into chuckling. He did too, still talking but also laughing. From that day to this, he never again spoke a harsh word to me. Once when I reported to him a serious error I'd made, one that really warranted a reprimand, he simply said, ***"You ain't s'posed to do that,"*** *and it was as effective as a chewing-out from anyone else.*

Last year, retired General Livsey, old and in poor health, was arrested for having not paid a food delivery man and then scuffled with him and with the police. I suspect alcohol was involved, mixed with embarrassment at having a debit card denied in front of his guests, the mixture then ignited by his temper. The whole overblown incident, an entertaining story to those who never really knew him, was a sad stain on the reputation of a man who had served his country long and well.

- "I, for one, will always look past the tempest in a teapot and remember the soldier I knew long ago."

CHAPTER V

The Epilogue

Let us now end this book and repeat the book's message in this epilogue. I will use General Livsey's writing style that begins with ***"tell 'um what you're gonna tell 'um,"*** then ***"tell 'um,"*** and ends with ***"tell 'um what you told 'um,"*** which is this part that summarizes the book messages.

1. THE PRIMARY MESSAGE IS TO ENCOURAGE AMERICAN CITIZENS TO VOTE AND CHOSE OUR LEADERS IN THE FORTHCOMING ELECTION.

a. We cannot defeat these enemies unless we understand that wars are fought in the Mind and from the Heavens as well as on Earth.

- The book warns about the dual threats to our nation and the world from Communism and radical Islam. The United States must resume its role as the leader of the free world and fight these enemies.

- We presented an education course involving a trip beyond our three-dimensional world to discover a Heavenly War Theater. ***If there's a Creator, or Good/God out there somewhere, then there's also an equal and opposite Destroyer, or Evil/Devil.*** The ***Heavenly*** powers engage in an ***eternal conflict*** to either provide for and protect us, or to fundamentally change and destroy us. The course further discusses 10 Lightning Bolts that can come at us either ***singularly*** or as a ***dual-edged*** bolt, with a ***good point*** on one side and a ***bad point*** on the opposite side. When this ***dual-edged*** Lightning Bolt ***hits,*** at times, we're not aware enough to know ***which point*** is affecting us.

b. We talked about the importance of citizens voting and cited Venezuela's 28 July 2024 Presidential election as an example of rigged elections.

The Year 2024 events in Venezuela demonstrated how important it is for citizens to have a voice in elections. **Nicolas Maduro** remains in power in Venezuela by using fraudulent voting techniques, and later forcing his political opponents into exile.

- ***"Exit polls"*** from voting booths after the 28 July 2024 Presidential elections showed former diplomat **Edmundo González Urrutia** receiving over 60% of the vote, however **Nicolas Maduro** declared himself the winner with 51% of the vote.

- The government-controlled **National Electoral Council** falsified results to show a narrow Maduro victory on 29 July 2024. They never provided the vote tallies to validate this election. **Maduro** later forced **Edmundo González Urrutia,** the real winner of the election, and his political opponents, to go into exile or hiding.

- There have been approximately 7 **million Venezuelans** who have fled communist rule of their nation during the Maduro regime. There is a forecasted additional **4-7 million** of **Venezuela's 28 million** population projected to flee Venezuela in the future if **Maduro** remains in power.

c. We compared how leaders in both the USA and Russia illegitimately subjugate their opponents to remain in power. The current USA regime censors and jails members of the opposition who question the legitimacy of the November 2020 election. They do this in order to impact the 2024 election. We also observed how assassinations of political leaders impact the governments of both Russia and the United States.

- **The Russians not only censor and jail opponents, but use assassinations to quell their opposition.** We cited 14 brutal examples of Russian assassination of opponents since Putin came to power in the Year 2000. This includes the worst of all, the 16 February 2024 murder of **Alexy Navalny. Navalny** was sentenced to 29 years in prison after he survived a Russian attempted assassination by poison in 2020. The Russian intelligence service and Vladimir Putin then murdered **Navalny** in the Siberian cell where he was imprisoned to permanently silence him.

- There have been two assassination attempts against former President Donald Trump in July and September 2024. The Florida governor, **Ron DeSantis,** is conducting a Florida-state probe into the 2nd assassination attempt that occurred in Palm Beach FL. The Florida state-run probe is partly due to a lack of confidence in the weaponized Federal Government to conduct a fair investigation into the assassination. *(reference the **"Lawfare"** activity by the Department of Justice against Donald Trump that we cited earlier in the book).*

- The similarities of prosecuting political opponents in Russia and the United States. We shared with you a 15 Feb 2024 comment from a reader ***"geopatriot"*** which summed up how leaders in Russia and the USA censor or eliminate their opposition. It is repeated here *(quote)*: ***"These Dems criticize the Russians for the same thing Biden has done to Trump and Conservatives in the USA since he became President, actually Biden is worse than Putin because we are supposed to live in freedom and democracy and free speech except if you are a conservative. Many Dems have questioned elections in the USA and no one on the left got charged. Everyone knows the 2020 election was rigged and the machines were hacked and states changed their voting laws before and during the elections in 2020. All over the world the leftist governments are destroying the lives of people and do not work for the people's best interests, but only for the politicians' interests or to make themselves richer. We are worse off than Russia."***

2. LEADERS MATTER AND ELECTIONS ARE CRUCIAL. This is the theme and also title of this book. We nominated seven LEADERS from the USA and Europe who chose to defy tyranny and oppose Communism/Marxism. They include **Field Marshall Erwin Rommel** from World War II and **General Bill Livsey** from the 20th Century Cold War. The three **LEADERS** from the USA who refused to surrender to the weaponized USA legal system are **Rudy Giuliani, Peter Navarro** and **Donald Trump**. We also nominated two from Russia to be **LEADERS**: **Alexei Navalny** (who is also a **Martyr for Freedom**); and his wife **Yulia Navalnaya** (with the hope that she can avoid becoming a **Martyr for Freedom**). Her words show she will continue the fight. ***"I have no right to give up. I will continue the work of Alexei Navalny. I will continue to fight for our country and I urge you to stand next to me. Putin killed not just the man Alexei Navalny, he wanted to kill our hope, our freedom, our future."***

That's all. This is the end of the book.
Thank you for reading it!

ABOUT THE AUTHOR

The author's 1968 photograph after his return from Vietnam

George Georgalis is a veteran of three wars, having served in 1967-68 Vietnam, as a civilian in the European Cold War from 1971-1986, and as an activated Army Reservist in the 1991 Gulf War. He is the author of ***"It's About Bridges, Vol IIB – The Education and War Stories***." That book compares nations to bridges, with both being vulnerable to destruction by crooked forces. It presents a theme that wars are fought in the mind and from the heavens as well as on Earth.

The attached photograph is the face of a dis-illusioned, bitter Vietnam veteran in 1968. He almost deserted the military during an Australia R&R to avoid returning to the ***"Tet-68 Offensive"*** campaign initiated by North Vietnam's **General Giap** on 30 January 1968. This confused Veteran witnessed the American military thoroughly defeat the Vietnam enemy in the January-March 1968 Tet-Offensive. He returned to the USA to observe how the media had grown tired of the USA involvement in 'Nam and was asserting that the USA, and not the North Vietnamese, were defeated.

He discovered the existence of a Mind War in Vietnam. He witnessed the 1968-1975 Mind War attack on the USA mainland which ultimately led to our withdrawal and abandonment of SE Asia to Communist aggressors, who subsequently massacred over 2 million civilians in Cambodia and Vietnam.

He found the Heavenly War Theater in the 1991 Gulf War and during the European Cold-War when Poland and Pope John Paul II influenced the miraculous destruction of the ***"Iron Curtain"*** separating Eastern

Europe from Freedom. He barely escaped with his wife and two children from Poland when the war that led to the liberation of Eastern Europe from Communism and the demise of the Soviet Union began on 13 December 1981. *(Note: The* ***"13th of December 1981"*** *is now a holiday in Poland, celebrating their liberation from Communism, much like the* ***"4th of July"*** *is a holiday celebrating the birth of Freedom in the USA).*

This book narrative is superimposed over an aerial view of the floating bridge connecting Cam Ranh Bay with the War Zone in mainland Vietnam, and the Dien Khanh "Bridge on the River Cai" crossing after it was completed on 4 Dec 1967. Nations are like Bridges. Our nation/bridge is threatened with destruction. This book helps us recognize the current threat which would transform our "One Nation Under God" into a Secular-Socialist society.

We cannot defeat this enemy that would destroy our Nation/Bridge unless we understand that wars are fought in the Mind and from the Heavens as well as on Earth. We are committed to this quest to defend our Nation. This is that story, and more importantly, why we need you to join in this venture if we are to defeat this most formidable enemy.

Printed in the USA
CPSIA information can be obtained
at www.ICGtesting.com
LVHW070545281024
794796LV00018B/311

9 798330 468881